George Canning Hill

Benjamin Franklin

A Biography

George Canning Hill

Benjamin Franklin
A Biography

ISBN/EAN: 9783337009656

Printed in Europe, USA, Canada, Australia, Japan

Cover: Foto ©Raphael Reischuk / pixelio.de

More available books at **www.hansebooks.com**

BENJAMIN FRANKLIN.

A Biography.

BY

GEORGE CANNING HILL

NEW YORK:
WORTHINGTON CO.,
747 BROADWAY.
1887.

CONTENTS.

CHAPTER I.

YOUTH AND APPRENTICESHIP, ... 1

CHAPTER II.

AT HIS TRADE, ... 34

CHAPTER III.

TO ENGLAND AND BACK, ... 59

CHAPTER IV.

IN BUSINESS, ... 81

CHAPTER V.

GETTING ALONG, ... 106

CHAPTER VI.

BECOMING A PUBLIC MAN, ... 129

CHAPTER VII.

GEORGE WHITFIELD—SOLDIERING—A PHILOSOPHER, . . . 152

1*   (v)

CHAPTER VIII.

GETTING FAME, ... 173

CHAPTER IX.

AS A MILITARY MAN, ... 199

CHAPTER X.

FIRST FIVE YEARS IN EUROPE, ... 224

CHAPTER XI.

FOREIGN AGENT OF THE COLONIES, ... 249

CHAPTER XII.

STEPS TO THE REVOLUTION, ... 271

CHAPTER XIII.

MINISTER TO FRANCE, ... 296

CHAPTER XIV.

CLOSE OF HIS CAREER, ... 317

BENJAMIN FRANKLIN.

CHAPTER I.

YOUTH AND APPRENTICESHIP.

IT is uncommon for the steps of so practical a person as Dr. Franklin to be turned into such romantic paths. He could have dreamed of nothing more than a life of hard and steady labor; yet the persevering pursuit of that very labor made him the counsellor of Generals and Congresses, the representative of his country at foreign Courts, and worthy to be asked to sit down with kings.

He was a genuine product of American soil. His mother-wit served him better than learning, and his ready knowledge of human nature was an invaluable resource. He was shrewd and sagacious; prudent, yet bold; frugal, yet generous; a student of philosophy, but a man of the world.

(7)

He took hold of whatever he did, that he might work out some tangible result. Nothing came to him by luck, but everything through labor. His instinctive modesty was only paralleled by his admirable self-possession. No man was ever more willing to keep himself out of sight, if by that means the cause could be helped on. He sought only stable things; and reputation followed as a matter of course. His clearness and coolness of judgment made him widely sought after as an adviser; and, if he offered a doubt, it was called one of "Franklin's portents," which led men to pause and reflect a little longer.

This is by no means a summary of his varied character, but a mere hint of the sterling ore which lay beneath.

Benjamin Franklin was born in Boston, but settled in business, at last, in Philadelphia, where he established his home. His father came over from England with his first wife, in 1685, bringing three children; four more were born to them in Boston, when his wife died, and he married again. The second wife bore him ten children, of which number Benjamin was the eighth, two girls being his juniors. The whole brood, therefore, counted seventeen: Franklin says, in his autobiography, that he remembered to have seen thirteen sitting around the table at one time.

His father's name was Josiah; he married Abiah Folger, a daughter of one of the early settlers of New England, whom old Cotton Mather styled "a godly and learned Englishman." His father's trade, after coming to New England, was that of a tallow-chandler and soap-boiler: he had been a dyer in the old country, but found that trade too poor an one to permit him to support his family. He was an excellent man, of a firm and healthy texture of character, fond of mechanical operations, skilled in drawing, and much given to music. After the day's work was over, he used to play on his violin, accompanying it with his voice. He was possessed of a sound judgment, and would have been called into public affairs had not his large family kept him in straitened circumstances and held him all the time close to his trade. His word, however, had weight with the leading men of his church, and many persons came to consult him about their private matters. They often chose him to decide in their differences, willing to abide his just decision. Franklin says that, at the family table, he liked to have some sensible friend, or neighbor, call in to converse with him,

and invariably started some topic for talk, with a
view to improve the minds of the children. "By
this means"—he adds—"he turned our attention
to what was good, just, and prudent, in the conduct of life; and little or no notice was ever taken
of what related to the victuals on the table, whether
it was well or ill dressed, in or out of season, of
good or bad flavor, preferable or inferior to this
or that other thing of the kind: so that I was
brought up in such a perfect inattention to those
matters, as to be quite indifferent what kind of
food was set before me."

Franklin's father lived to be eighty-nine years
of age, and his mother to be eighty-five: he says
he never knew either of them to have any sickness but that of which they died. They lie buried
in Boston, where he erected over them a marble
tablet, on which is recorded the story of their
lives and virtues. The inscription on this stone
is curious enough to be copied into even the
briefest life of the dutiful and illustrious son.
This is it:—

JOSIAH FRANKLIN

and

Abiah his wife,

Lie here interred.

They lived lovingly together in wedlock

Fifty-five years;

And without an estate, or any gainful employment,

By constant labor, and honest industry,

(With God's blessing,)

Maintained a large family comfortably,

And brought up thirteen children, and seven grandchildren

Reputably.

From this instance, reader,

Be encouraged to diligence in thy calling,

And distrust not Providence.

He was a pious and prudent man,

She a discreet and virtuous woman.

Their youngest son,

In filial regard to their memory,

Places this stone.

J. F. born 1655; died 1744, Æt. 89.

A. F. born 1667; died 1752, Æt. 85.

When young Benjamin was eight years old, he was sent to the grammar school, his father meaning to devote him to the service of the church. The lad was a ready learner, and made rapid progress in his classes, rising from one to another. He was kept here but about a year, however, his father's circumstances not allowing him to think

of sending him to college, and was next put to a
Mr. George Brownwell, who kept a famous school
for writing and arithmetic. With this teacher he
soon learned to write a good hand; but he confesses that he made a failure in his arithmetic!
He was but ten years old, when his father took
him out of school to help him in his business of
tallow-chandler and soap-boiler; and the future
philosopher and statesman was, so early in life as
that, cutting wicks for candles, filling moulds with
melted tallow, waiting on the shop, and running
of errands. He declares that he did not like the
trade, and wanted to go to sea; but his father
would permit no such thing. Living where the
tides came and went twice each day, he spent
more or less time about the water, and very soon
learned to swim well, and to manage boats; and
when the least trouble threatened the young crew
on the water, Franklin was set up as captain and
controller.

He was generally a leader among his comrades,
and admits that he sometimes led them into
"scrapes;" he mentions one such, to show what
spirit he was made of. "There was a salt marsh,"
he says, "which bounded part of the mill-pond,
on the edge of which, at high water, we used to

stand to fish for minnows. By much trampling we had made it a mere quagmire. My proposal was to build a wharf there for us to stand upon, and I showed my comrades a large heap of stones which were intended for a new house near the marsh, and which would very well suit our purpose. Accordingly, in the evening, when the workmen were gone home, I assembled a number of my playfellows, and we worked diligently, like so many emmets, sometimes two or three to a stone, till we brought them all to make a little wharf. The next morning, the workmen were surprised at missing the stones, which had formed our wharf. Inquiry was made after the authors of this transfer; we were discovered, complained of, and *corrected by our fathers;* and, though I demonstrated the utility of our work, mine convinced me that that which was not *honest,* could not be truly *useful.*"

Franklin continued with his father in the soap boiler's business for two years, arriving at his twelfth year. He disliked the trade worse than ever; and his father began to fear lest the lad would indeed run away to sea, if his own wishes in the matter of a calling were not more regarded. So he took his son to walk with him all about the town, among the joiners, the bricklayers, the

2

turners, the braziers, and the men of other trades
and occupations, while at their work, all the time
watching to see which of them all the lad might
appear to prefer, and intending to let him choose
any one of them, if that would only break his
tendency for the sea.   One happy result came of
these repeated visits, if no other: when the boy
became a man, he knew so much of the several
trades, and how workmen handled their tools, that
he was always ready to perform trifling jobs in
the house, and could construct machines for his
philosophical experiments just when his intention
was fresh and warm in his mind.

His father at last designed him for the cutler's
trade, and placed him for a few days, as a trial,
with his brother Samuel, who had been bred to
the trade in London, and had recently set up in
business in Boston; but his cousin demanded so
large a fee for his apprenticeship, that his father
was displeased with it, and the lad was taken
home again.   A single circumstance at this point
came in to decide the whole matter; owing to
this alone, Benjamin Franklin was put in the way
of becoming widely useful to his own generation,
and illustrious before the world.   *He had a passion
for reading.*   That was the golden key which un-

locked his whole future. All the money he could earn he spent in buying books. He took especial delight in voyages. The first books he bought were Bunyan's works, in small volumes. These he afterwards sold, to get the money to buy R. Burton's "Historical Collections," in all, forty little volumes. He read the greater part of his father's library, which was made up of volumes on theology, and was of a dry, argumentative character. He said he had often regretted that at that particular time more proper books had not been thrown in his way, especially as he was not to study afterward for the ministry. He found Plutarch's Lives among his father's books, and devoured them; many a promising lad has done it before and since, and Franklin confessed the great benefit he received from the book. He mentions, likewise, a book written by De Foe, styled an "Essay on Projects," and one, in particular, written by the famous Cotton Mather, called "An Essay to do Good." Much and lasting good it did in his case, certainly. He admitted that it gave him "a turn of thinking," and had an influence on some of the future events of his life.

Seeing how he liked books and reading, his

father resolved to make him a printer. This was
the long and decisive step in his career. One son,
James, was already of that trade, and had returned
from England not a long time before, with press
and other implements, to set up business in Boston. Benjamin admits that he liked the idea of
that trade much better than his father's, although
he could not yet wholly give up the sea. To
make it secure as soon as possible, his father
made haste to bind him to service to the elder
brother. Benjamin resisted the plan for some
time, but was at length persuaded, and put his
own name to the legal indenture, being but
twelve years old at the time of doing it. This
instrument held him to serve his brother James,
at the printer's trade, until he should become
twenty-one years old; but, according to custom,
he was to have journeyman's wages the last year.

IIe took hold in earnest, and made such progress at his new trade that he was soon of real
value to his brother's business. In his new situation he was thrown in the way of procuring better
books, and more of them. A friendship con-
tracted with the booksellers' apprentices of the
town enabled him, from time to time, to borrow
a small volume, which he always returned soon,

and clean. Other borrowers might take a useful hint from their great exemplar, and save a great deal of hard feeling. He used to sit up in his chamber, very often for the greater part of the night, reading, so as to return in the morning the book he had borrowed the evening before, lest it should be missed from the bookseller's shop. There was a merchant in Boston then, Matthew Adams by name, who was in the habit of calling in at the printing office of James Franklin; he had a good store of books, and, seeing how fond the printer lad was of reading, generously invited him to come and see his library, offering to lend him whatever books he wanted to read.

He tried his hand at writing poetry about this time, and his brother rather encouraged him to continue with it; he composed a couple of ballads, one of them called "The Light House Tragedy," and the other a sailor's song, on the capture of one Teach, a pirate of the day, who was nicknamed "Blackbeard." Franklin himself afterward admitted that they were "wretched stuff." When they were printed, his brother sent him around town to peddle them. Of the former he sold a very large number, and he was made somewhat vain in consequence; but his father, who

2*

had good hard sense, criticised his ballads without
mercy, and wound up with telling him that
"versemakers were generally beggars." This ut-
terly discouraged the youth's ambition in that
direction. He says he "escaped being a poet,
and probably a very bad one."

All this, however, had no effect to dissuade
him from his resolution to acquire skill in expressing his thoughts in good *prose*. There was a lad
in town named John Collins, who was a close
friend of young Franklin. Both loved to argue,
and were fond of disputing, although Franklin
admitted when he grew wiser that it was a bad
habit in a man, and very apt to spoil conversation,
to sour friendship, and to disgust the company;
he afterward observed that few persons were ad-
dicted to it beside lawyers and collegians. Collins and himself became concerned in an argument about the propriety of educating females,
and their natural ability for study; his friend
professing to believe the other sex intellectually
inferior to ours, and Franklin maintaining the
contrary. Collins rather vanquished the future
philosopher with the greater flow of his words,
while the latter still remained unconvinced by his
reasons. To place the matter on its merits solely,

after they separated, Franklin put down *his* arguments on paper, in as clear phrases as he could
command, and copied and sent them to his opponent. Collins read and answered them, and Franklin replied. They had been disputing in this style
to the number of three or four letters, when the
lad's father chanced to come across *his* papers, and
read them. Soon afterward, he sat down and
talked with his son about what he had discovered;
he did not offer to argue the question involved,
either one way or another, but he touched upon
his son's style of writing, observing that, although
he clearly had the advantage of his opponent in
punctuation and spelling, he fell far short of him
in style of expression, in clearness, and in his
method of discussion. The criticism came in
good time; it set the youth to thinking on the
faults of his composition, and aroused his resolution to make himself a clear and effective writer.

He fell in with an odd volume of the British
"Spectator," then,—a happy coincidence indeed.
It was the first time he had ever seen any part of
those delightful essays. He bought the volume,
and read it again and again with much delight.
He liked its easy style of writing so well, that he
resolved to try and imitate it. To this end, he

began with a single number, or essay, in the volume; mastering the thoughts or sentiments of each
sentence, and noting them down on paper, he laid
them by for a few days, and then put them in the
best language of his own which he could command, and compared what he had done with what
the writers of the "Spectator" had done. In this
way, he was really writing up to the "Spectator"
standard, the famous authors of that collection of
essays furnishing him with criticisms, hints, and
models, as he went along. In no other way could
he so readily detect his own faults, or hope to
correct them. This plan he pursued with industry for some time, and had the satisfaction of
seeing his own improvement. To gain a wider
command of words, he turned some of the "Spectator's" tales into verse; and afterwards, when he
had quite forgotten the "Spectator's" prose,
turned them back again into prose of his own.

In order to exercise his mind in the art of
methodizing and arranging his subjects as they
came up for treatment, he would mix up the hints
he had jotted down on paper, and some time afterward endeavor to arrange them for himself, so as
to present them in the most obvious order and
with the greatest force. He labored hard at his

self-imposed tasks in English composition, but he was resolved to become "a tolerable English writer," and persevered until he met with success. He was helping himself to an education; many a youth of his years refuses to do anything for his own improvement, when he has everybody to help him. The time he devoted to this kind of self-instruction, as well as to his reading, was either at night or before going to work in the morning; on Sundays, too, he went quietly to the printing office, preferring not to attend public worship, and there gave the day to his reading and writing exercises. His father would have expected him to attend church, if he had been living at home; but being apprenticed to his brother, he had in a measure passed beyond the reach of parental restraints. He acknowledges that he considered going to church to be a duty, but that he could not afford time to practice it.

Time passed, the apprentice closely pursuing his studies and his work. When he was sixteen, he fell in with a book that recommended a vegetable diet, and determined to make an experiment of that style of living. His brother was not a married man, and was therefore compelled to board out his apprentices. It made trouble in the family arrangements for one apprentice to decline eating meat, and Franklin read his vegetarian work more carefully, to learn how to cook the various dishes he wanted for himself; in a short time he qualified himself to make hasty puddings and other sorts of puddings, to boil rice and potatoes, and to cook many other simple dishes. Then he went to his brother and made the following proposal,—if the latter would give him each week only half the amount he paid for his board, he would undertake to board himself! This from a boy of sixteen! His brother readily accepted a proposal like that; and even out of that half allowance, Franklin saved still a half, with which he purchased books. He also saved the time he otherwise would have taken in going from the office to his meals, and returning. While his brother and the rest of the apprentices were gone, he ate his frugal meal, often consisting of no more than a biscuit, or a slice of bread, or a tart, and a glass of water, and then applied himself to study until their return. He felt his head to be clearer and his apprehension much quicker, from practising this temperance. In these odd scraps of time, snatched from his meals, he resolutely studied Arithmetic, of which

he felt that he was wretchedly ignorant, and proceeded some way into Navigation. He likewise
read at this time so deep a book as "Locke on
Human Understanding," and another entitled
"The Art of Thinking." English Grammar he
took up, too; and an article on Logic, at the end
of the book out of which he studied, led him to
an acquaintance with the writings of Socrates,
and especially with the mode adopted by that
philosopher of arguing topics, which was by asking questions like an humble inquirer. In consequence of this acquaintance with the Greek sage,
he dropped his former style of arguing with
positive denial and plump dogmatism, and took
to the "Socratic Method," which he followed
ever after, and found it of the widest use and
efficacy. Instead of arousing those with whom
he did not agree to open antagonism, he put
them questions which would draw them out in
definitions and concessions,—they not seeing
whither his questions tended,—and then obtained
his victory by their own help. He thought sometimes that neither his cause nor himself was
fairly entitled to such victories.

His improvement now was rapid and percept-
ible. He could not have failed to make progress,

with this thorough self-searching. About the year 1720, his brother published a newspaper, the second that had been printed in America. It was called the "New England Courant." His friends tried to dissuade him from such a project, thinking that one newspaper was enough for the country; but he persevered, and young Benjamin was employed as a carrier to the subscribers. He would first work at the types, then at the press, and finally carry around the paper. Seeing that some persons whom he knew began to contribute short articles to the "Courant," the ambitious carrier conceived the bold idea of writing for its columns too. He was afraid his brother James would refuse to admit any article which he knew to be his, so he artfully disguised his hand, wrote his communication, and placed it under the door over night. In the morning it was picked up, and submitted to those who were in the habit of dropping in and passing judgment on the articles written. Franklin was greatly pleased to listen to their favorable criticisms, and especially to hear them guess what respectable man of the town might be the author! This unexpected success so pleased him that he resolved to begin and write for the press regularly,

taking all the pains possible with his productions.
He kept his secret well until his "fund of sense,"
as he styled it, was exhausted, and then he made
himself known to his friends as the real author
about whom they had indulged so many sur-
mises.

His brother James, however, did not seem to
like it so well, and perhaps thought Ben. would
be made vain by the good opinions of others; and
it is recorded that with this circumstance the
trouble between the two brothers began. James
felt that he was the *master* of Benjamin, because
the latter had been bound out to him after. legal
forms; while Benjamin thought that, even if he
were apprenticed to his brother, the latter should
have given him kinder treatment, *because* he was
his brother. When they fell into disputes,—
which came to be pretty often,—their troubles
were carried before their father, to whom each
pleaded his own case; and Benjamin having the
decision made in his favor pretty often, this fact
only served to widen instead of to heal the
breach between them. Ben. began to feel the
weight of the yoke of his apprenticeship, and to
wish it lifted from his neck altogether. At any
rate, the tyrannical treatment from which he then

suffered, excited his hatred of tyranny from that
time forward through his whole career.

About this time, or very soon after, an article
in the Franklin newspaper gave great offence to
the Massachusetts Assembly. James was arrested
by warrant of the Speaker of the House, publicly
censured by him, and then thrown into prison for
a month, because he would not make known the
writer of the offensive article.

Benjamin was likewise arrested and brought before the Governor's Council; he was merely ad-
monished by them, probably not being thought
responsible for the fault, inasmuch as he was but
an apprentice. While his brother James lay in
prison, of course he had the management of the
paper; he confesses that he "made bold to give
our rulers *some rubs* in it," which his brother was
not at all displeased with, but which led to his
being considered by others as "a youth that had
a turn for libelling and satire." When his brother
was at length discharged, it was ordered by the
assembly that "*James Franklin* should no longer
print the newspaper called ' *The New England
Courant.*'" It was talked over among the friends
of the paper what was best to do; some were for
changing its name, so that "James Franklin"

could go on with its management; but as that course would be attended with some inconveniences, it was finally resolved to let the paper be continued under its old name, with *Benjamin Franklin* as its manager and controller. In order to make the whole transaction legal and fair, James returned to Benjamin his indenture, with a full discharge written on the back of it, which could be exhibited in case of threatened trouble. But Benjamin was nevertheless to sign new papers, binding himself to his brother for the remainder of his time; all these were to be kept private. And in this way the "New England Courant" was printed by Benjamin Franklin for several months; thus was the youth launched on the open sea where he was to gain a livelihood and a name.

Pretty soon a fresh quarrel broke out between the brothers. Benjamin declared he would leave, and produced his elder brother's discharge, written on the back of the original indenture, as clear proof of his right to do so. He dared his brother to show the *private* agreement to anybody, well knowing its worthlessness. Franklin confessed that this was clearly wrong, as taking an unfair advantage; but he said he was provoked to it by the blows which his brother dealt out on him in one of his many fits of passion. James Franklin, however, was not at other times an ill-natured man, Benjamin says; "perhaps," added he, very candidly, " I was too saucy and provoking."

They separated at once, after that; but James took care to go around to the other printing offices in town, and influence the masters not to give Benjamin work; and it was this single circumstance that drove him so far from his friends as New York, at first, and afterward to Philadelphia. He did not feel as bad about turning his back on Boston either, as he otherwise might, had he not come under the displeasure of the Government by the course of his newspaper; and he said he feared, too, that if he stayed there longer, he would "soon bring himself into scrapes." He was looked upon by many persons already as "an infidel and an atheist," because of his disputes on religious matters.

His father, however, took sides now with his elder brother, and would have kept him at home in Boston until his indenture regularly expired. This led the youth to take the resolution to *run away*. His friend Collins, with whom he used to debate questions on paper, aided him in his purpose. Collins made an agreement for him with the captain of a sloop, bound for New York, to take him on board, saying that he was a young man of his acquaintance who had got into trouble with a girl of bad reputation, and who her parents insisted should marry her; in consequence of which, he could neither make his appearance in public, nor come down to his vessel except privately. To raise the money needed to defray his passage, Franklin sold some of his books, and was taken on board without the knowledge of any one. With a favorable wind he was on the water but three days, at the end of which time he found himself in the streets of New York, three hundred miles from home, but seventeen years of age, knowing no one in the whole place, bearing no letter of recommendation to any person, and with as little money as possible in his pocket. This was in October, in the year 1723.

Benjamin Franklin now had his own way to make. He chanced to be one of the few runaway lads who "came to something" afterwards.

He was by this time pretty well cured of his propensity for the sea, and began to look around for work to do. There was a Mr. William Bradford in town, a printer, who had come from Philadelphia not long before in consequence of a

3 *

quarrel with the Pennsylvania Governor, and to
him young Franklin forthwith presented himself.
The kind stranger received him in a friendly
manner, told him he could give him nothing to
do there, but suggested that he might find a place
at Philadelphia with his son, whose best hand had
recently died. Franklin was grateful enough for
the hint, and immediately set about acting on it.
He went on board a boat at once for Amboy,
leaving directions for his chest to come round by
sea after him. His boating experience was un-
pleasant, a squall overtook them, tore in pieces
their wretched sails, and drove them on Long
Island. A drunken Dutchman fell overboard,
whom Franklin pulled out of the water by the
hair of his head. The fellow drew a book out of
his pocket, and asked the lad to dry it for him;
Franklin was delighted to find it was his dear old
friend, John Bunyan, "in Dutch, finely printed on
good paper, copper cuts, and a dress better than
he had ever seen it wear in its own language." A
printer's eye for everything, The little craft lay
at anchor off the Island all that day and the following night, the sea rolling so that it was impossible
to get help from the shore. They all crowded in
under the hatches that night, wet and hungry and

feverish; the next day, however, the wind shifted, and by night they reached Amboy. They had been thirty hours on the water, without anything to eat, and with no drink but a bottle of rum.

Franklin had taken cold and felt fever upon him. He had somewhere read of copious draughts of water being efficient to break up a fever, and resolved to try the remedy. During the night he sweat profusely, and felt so much better in the morning as to be able to set out on foot, after crossing by the ferry, for Burlington, a distance of fifty miles; there he expected to find conveyance by water to Philadelphia. The homeless boy had hard luck of it. It began to rain, and kept raining all day long; so that he was really soaked before he had gone many miles, and obliged, by noon, feeling extremely tired too, to call at a wayside tavern for lodgings, where he rested himself for the night. He became now very homesick, and many times wished he had never thought of leaving home. The people in the house asked him a good many close questions, and he began to fear lest he should be thought what he really was,—a runaway apprentice, and apprehended and sent back whence he came. But he pushed on the next morning, and walked that day to within ten miles of Burlington, stopping for the night at a house kept by Dr. Brown, an infidel, who became much interested in talking on various subjects with him.

Next morning he started for Burlington. He arrived there to find the regular boats to Philadelphia just gone. It was then Saturday, and no more were to leave until Tuesday. He went straight back to an old woman in Burlington of whom he had purchased gingerbread on his arrival, and asked her frankly what was best to do. She offered to lodge him until the next regular boat left; and on afterwards finding out that he was a printer by trade, she tried to induce him to stay there and pursue his craft. She was exceedingly kind to the youth, giving him some ox-cheek for his dinner, and making him as contented as she knew how. While he chanced to be strolling by the river side at evening, a boat drew near, having several passengers aboard. He was told she was bound for Philadelphia, and asked the boatmen to take him aboard. There was no wind, and they were obliged to tug at the oars all the way. They even pulled past the city, not knowing they had reached it. A little past midnight some of the passengers raised the question whether they had not gone by; the result of the dispute was, they put the boat toward the shore, worked into a creek, made fast to an old fence from which they took the rails to build a fire, and stayed there until the light of morning revealed the truth to their eyes. They *were* beyond Philadelphia, as some of them supposed. Immediately they got the boat out from the creek and pulled back for the town; where they arrived between eight and nine o'clock.

Franklin landed on Market street wharf on a Sunday morning, in his working clothes, dirty from the long voyage, his pockets stuffed out with shirts and stockings, and himself a stranger to everybody, and knowing not where to go to seek a lodging.

CHAPTER II.

AT HIS TRADE.

IN such plight he entered the city where he was to lay the foundation of his future fame, and live to enjoy its most satisfying rewards. He had one dollar in his pocket beside a shilling's worth of copper coins. The latter he gave to the boatmen for bringing him from Burlington; they refused to take it, because he had rowed his way along; but he persisted until they took what he offered. Walking along the street, he met a lad with bread, and asked where he got it; being directed to a baker's, he at once entered the shop and called for some biscuit, thinking the bakers of Philadelphia made up their bread after the same patterns and styles with their brethren of Boston. The baker kept no such article as biscuit. He then called for a three penny loaf, but the baker had nothing like that. Finally, bidding the man give him three cents' worth of such bread as

he had, he received " three great puffy rolls," as
he afterwards described them, and walked off.
His pockets being filled with dirty clothes, as
already mentioned, he put a roll under each arm,
and ate the third as he strolled up the streets. In
this style he walked up Market to Fourth street,
and chanced to pass the house of a Mr. Read,
whose daughter Sarah, whom he afterwards married, was standing in the door, amused with the
awkward appearance of the youth.

Reaching Fourth street, he turned and walked
down Chestnut and part of Walnut streets, still
engaged with his "puffy" roll, and came around
at last at the wharf whence he started. He went
on board the boat he had come on, and got some
water to wash his bread down; and finding a
woman, with her child, still on board, waiting to
go on, he gave her the remaining two rolls, and
felt as if he had done his duty. Once more he
sallied forth up the street. Large numbers of
persons were thronging the walks, and he fell in
with the current, willing to go wherever it might
take him. He was borne into the Quaker Meeting-House, near the Market, where he sat down
in the midst of the silent worshippers, and, hearing not a word spoken for a long time, finally fell

asleep. Nor did he awake until aroused by a
person who told him services were over, and the
house was to be shut up. This Quaker meeting-
house afforded him the first sleep he got in
Philadelphia. It overpowered him, he was so
worn down with excessive labor, fasting, and
watchfulness, since he left New York.

On the way down to the river again, he fell in
with a young Quaker whose face he liked, and
ventured to ask him about a good tavern, where
a stranger could get lodgings. "Here," said the
Quaker, pointing to the sign of the Three
Mariners' tavern, hard by, "is a house where
they receive strangers, but it is not a reputable
one; if thee wilt walk with me, I'll show thee a
better one." The Quaker showed him to the
sign of the "Crooked Billet," in Water street.
This, therefore, was Franklin's first hostelry in
the City of Brotherly Love. He took his dinner
there, and began to be afraid, from the questions
put him, that his character would be suspected.

After dinner, completely tired out, he asked to
be shown to bed, and laid himself down on it
without removing his clothes; there he slept till
six o'clock, when he was called to supper. Soon
after supper, he went to bed again, and slept

without waking until morning. He needed the copious rest he was taking. Dressing himself neatly, he went over to the printing office of Mr. William Bradford's son, to solicit work. Whom should he find there but the same Mr. Bradford he had met in New York,—the old gentleman having come on horseback and arrived before him. He introduced young Franklin to his son, who invited him to take breakfast with him. The younger Bradford was not then in want of a hand in the office, but he told the youth of another printer, who had lately set up business, and who would perhaps employ him. The name of the new printer was Keimer. At any rate, Mr. Bradford assured him that, if he did not get work there, he might lodge at his house, and he would give him a little work, now and then, which might help along until something better offered.

Mr. Bradford, senior, went at once with Franklin to Keimer's office, and introduced him thus · "Neighbor," said he, "I have brought to see you a young man of your business; perhaps you may want such a one." Keimer put the youth a few questions, handed him a "composing stick," to see how he could work, and at once promised to

4

give him employment, though just then he had
nothing for him to do. The office was wretchedly stocked, for which a beginner in the business might have abundant excuse. Franklin
went to lodge and board at Bradford's for a time,
until Keimer should send for him to work off a
poem he was then setting up from his miserable
stock of types. He had ingeniously put the
press in working order for him already. In a
little time, Keimer found something for him to
do. Both the printers of the town were but poor
workmen, and had a meagre stock of cases, types,
and machinery, with which to pursue their occupation. Franklin had an ambition to master his
trade, and excel every one about him engaged in
it. Bradford was an illiterate man, while Keimer
was somewhat of a scholar; the latter Franklin
found to be more or less knavish. He did not
like to have the lad lodge at Bradford's while he
worked for *him*, but he had no accommodation
for him at his own house, and finally arranged
the matter by procuring him lodgings at the
house of Mr. Read, the same man in whose door
he passed the young lady as he went along the
street eating his roll. His chest of clothes had
come round from New York by this time, and he

said he now made a more respectable appearance in her eyes than when eating his bread.

Here he lived, working industriously and making himself contented. He tried to forget Boston entirely, and let none of his friends there know of his whereabouts, save Collins. He saved his money, and began to lay the foundations of his success. One day, his brother-in-law, named Robert Holmes, who was captain of a coaster that plied between Boston and Delaware, happening to hear of Benjamin while he was below at New Castle, wrote him a letter, telling him of the grief of his friends at his long absence, pledging himself that they all felt kindly toward him, and begging him to return to them without delay. Franklin replied to his letter; but he told *his* story in so different a light that his relative changed his opinion very greatly of the cause and circumstances of the lad's sudden departure. As it happened, too, Governor Keith was at New Castle at the time, and in company with Captain Holmes when Franklin's letter arrived. The latter showed it to the Governor, who read it, asked the lad's age, and expressed his astonishment. He thought him a boy of great promise, who deserved to be encouraged; spoke of what poor printers there were in Philadelphia, and held up the idea of Franklin's starting in business for himself. He promised, for his part, to procure the public business for him, and to help him in every way he could.

Governor Keith's connection with the young craftsman was of a strange character, resulting in no sort of profit. Not long after this trifling occurrence at New Castle, the Governor came directly over to Keimer's, the latter hurrying down stairs, filled with the idea that he was to receive a call of importance. But great was his chagrin to hear his Excellency inquire for young Franklin. The Governor came up, offered the lad a profusion of civilities and compliments, blamed him very much for not having made himself known before, and, right before the face of Keimer, invited him to go to a tavern and taste some madeira with him. Franklin said he was as much astonished as Keimer could have been; however, to the tavern he went, and there the Governor opened his plan for him over the madeira. He would have the youth set up in business forthwith; he offered him all the assistance possible; a gentleman with him from Delaware also offered to get as much of the business from that government as he could; and it appeared as if fortune had come in for him at flood tide

The lad expressed doubts as to how his father would view the matter, for on him he would have to rely for aid in stocking his office; but the Governor promised to give him a letter to his father, explaining the whole project, and especially setting forth its advantages. He thought it all over well, and then resolved to return home at once and see his father. It was kept a secret in the meantime, however, and he remained at work with Keimer as before. Now and then, he was invited to go and dine with the Governor, an honor which he duly prized. A little vessel was up for Boston, about the last of April. Franklin took his leave of Keimer, saying merely that he was going home to see his friends. The Governor gave him his letter, as he had promised, and in it showed the lad's father what an opportunity there was for the latter to make his fortune in Philadelphia.

The passage to Boston consumed two weeks. The vessel ran on a shoal going down the bay, and sprung a leak; the weather was rough after they got to sea, and Franklin took his turn at the pumps with the rest. It was seven months since he ran away from Boston, in which time his friends had not heard a syllable of him; for his

4*

brother-in-law Holmes had not yet got back, and
he had written nothing of him, either. The family
were vastly surprised at his return; yet they were
all glad enough to see him, save his brother
James. Benjamin went over to his printing office
to see him; he was much better clad than when
he used to work for him, having a new suit of
clothes on, a watch in his pocket, and nearly five
pounds in money. Franklin said his brother
looked him all over, and turned to his work
again. The hands in the office asked him all
manner of questions; what kind of a *country* it
was where he had been, and how he liked it.
One of them wanted to know what sort of money
they had there; whereupon Franklin drew out
from his well-lined pocket a handful of silver
coins, and spread it out temptingly before them.
It was a new sight for them, paper being the only
money used in Boston at that time. He pulled
out his watch and showed them, too; and finally,
he gave them a dollar to drink, and took his leave
of them all. His brother was sullen and silent all
the while; in fact, he was very mad about the
visit; and when their mother afterward spoke to
him of being reconciled to Benjamin, he declared
in most violent language that he never would be

reconciled to him in the world, for he had been insulted before his workmen by the runaway in a manner which he could never forget nor forgive. But the younger brother lived to do the elder a good turn, in after years, and to assist him when he most needed help, and when it was most welcome.

He handed Governor Keith's letter to his father, which occasioned the latter a still greater surprise. About this time, too, Capt. Holmes arrived home, and the father read the letter to him, inquiring very particularly of Sir William Keith, and expressing his astonishment that he should have thus offered to befriend a youth, who would not come to man's estate for three years. Holmes said all he could in favor of Keith and the project, but it did not influence the strong judgment of the parent; he set his face against the whole plan, and at once sat down and wrote a letter to the Governor, politely thanking him for the interest he had seen fit to take in his son, but positively declining to give him any aid at that time in beginning business for himself; he said he was much too young to undertake the responsibilities of business, and it would require a good deal of money, too, which a youth was not yet prepared to manage.

His father would not deny, however, that he was pleased with the marks of attention shown the son; and he readily consented to his return to Philadelphia, especially as there was such deep-seated ill feeling toward him on his brother's part, and he had already shown how well he could do when left to swim for himself. His father gave him some good advice before he went; enjoining him "to behave respectfully to the people there, endeavor to obtain the general esteem, and avoid lampooning and libelling," to which he thought the young man was too much inclined. He assured him that, if he was prudent, by the time he became one-and-twenty he might save enough to set himself up in business; and that if he should have nearly enough money for that purpose, but not quite enough, he would then make up the difference to him. This was all his father would then do for him. His parents both presented him with little gifts, as tokens of their affection, and he left home again, embarking for New York. This time he went with their blessings and prayers.

The vessel put in at Newport, where Benjamin

called to see his brother John, who was settled there. He was received very cordially, having always been a favorite with this brother. An acquaintance of this brother, named Vernon, learning that Benjamin was going to Philadelphia, and having a debt of thirty-five pounds due him in Pennsylvania, requested him to collect it there, and keep the money until it should be called for. This money afterwards gave him considerable anxiety, from the fact, that when he had collected it he appropriated a great part of it to his own use, and then felt troubled lest he should any day be called on for it.

Setting sail from Newport, the vessel received on board several passengers; among them, a Quaker lady, with her servants, and a couple of young women who appeared to be travelling together. Franklin, young as he was, and unacquainted with the ways of worldly persons, became somewhat familiar with these two young women, which excited the attention of the Quaker lady; and as she had already held a little conversation with him on other matters, she ventured to break her mind to him on this. Taking him aside, therefore, she said in a kind manner, — "Young man, I am concerned for thee, as thou hast no friend with thee, and seems not to knc w much of the world, or of the snares youth is exposed to; depend upon it, these are very bad women; I can see it by all their actions; and if thee art not upon thy guard, they will draw thee into some danger; they are strangers to thee; and I advise thee, in a friendly concern for thy welfare, to have no acquaintance with them." The youth was surprised; but she told him of some things which she had seen and heard, and he was soon convinced she knew best about it. The girls told him where they lived, as soon as they reached New York, and invited him to come and see them; but he was careful not to go near them, wisely remembering the Quaker lady's warnings. The day after, the captain of the vessel missed several articles from the cabin; the rooms of these women were searched by an officer, and the stolen property found upon them. They were punished as common thieves.

His friend Collins, whom he met on this visit home, had started for Philadelphia before him, and got as far as New York. When Franklin reached the latter city, he found him already there. Collins, however, had fallen into a drinking habit since Franklin's first absence from home, a matter which his friend greatly deplored; and when the latter saw him once more on his arrival in New York, he found that he had been drunk every day since landing. He had gambled too, and thus lost all his money : so that Franklin was obliged to loan him enough to discharge the cost of his passage to Philadelphia. Collins was a man of parts, and very well read.

The Governor of New York, whose name was Burnet,—a son of the famous Bishop Burnet, of England,—had heard of a passenger's being on board who had a supply of books, and asked the captain to bring him to him. Franklin went along to answer this *second* gubernatorial requisition, but declined taking his friend Collins with him, on account of his sad condition. The Governor received the youthful printer with great civility, showed him into his library, and began to talk very familiarly on books and authors. It was a compliment which young Franklin appreciated.

He went on with his journey to the city of his adoption. On the way, he collected Mr. Vernon's debt; and glad enough, too, was he of the funds, for he could not have got along without them. He tried to help Collins to a situation, but those

to whom he applied saw what his unfortunate
habits were, and declined employing him. Then
Collins began to pester Franklin for money; he
knew the latter had the Vernon debt about him,
and that encouraged him to borrow. He promised, of course, to pay all back when he got
into business, and in this way took up the larger
part of it.

Collins was sailing with his friend Franklin
and others, on the Delaware, one day, and, being
more or less intoxicated, refused very crossly to
do anything to help to propel the boat. He
declared, however, that he would be rowed
home; but Franklin as stoutly declared that
they would *not* row him. Said Collins, in reply,
"You must row me, or stay all night on the
water,—as you please." The rest were ready to
give up to him; but Franklin was resolved to do
no such thing, and he persisted in his refusal.
Upon this, Collins swore he would *make* him
row; and, clambering along over the others to
reach him, he came up and struck out at him!
Just at the right instant, Franklin placed his
head under the fellow's legs, and then rising up
in his seat, threw him heels over head into the
river! He was an excellent swimmer, and that

Franklin knew; therefore, he gave his mind little anxiety about the result. When the victim had managed to swim around, and got ready to lay his hand on the side of the boat to draw himself in, the rowers fetched a vigorous pull with their oars and put the boat clear of his reach. So it was several times; whenever he would swim up and get all ready to lay hold, away went the boat again. He grew even more incensed than before, and, in answer to frequent inquiries, obstinately declared that he would not row at all. He became so tired at length that it was thought prudent to draw him in again; wet and out of temper, he cut but a sorry figure. But it was the last of Franklin's acquaintance with his old and early friend; they had little to say to one another after that. The poor fellow went out to the West Indies, not long afterwards, as a preceptor for the sons of a gentleman at Barbadoes. He promised Franklin he would remit for the money he had borrowed of him, from the first of his own receipts; but the latter never heard a word more from him, nor received back a single pound of the borrowed money.

Franklin's reflection on this occurrence, on looking it all over and seeing how he acted with

5

Mr. Vernon's money, was this: it was one of the
first great errors of his life; and his father knew
better than he did himself that he was yet too
young to undertake the responsibilities of business and the management of money.

Governor Keith still followed him up, notwithstanding the decision of his father. He told him
to make out an inventory of the articles he would
want in order to furnish a shop, and show it to
him. Franklin had kept Keith's advances a
secret from Keimer and everybody else, up to
this time; had he confided in any second person,
he might have got advice in the matter which
would have materially aided him. But he could
not suspect that such generous offers were in the
least insincere. Accordingly, he sat down and
drew up his little inventory, making the cost of
it amount to one hundred pounds sterling,—or
about five hundred dollars. The Governor expressed himself pleased with the result, and then
turned and asked Franklin if it would not be
better for him to be on the ground himself when
these articles were purchased, so that he could
select his types and see to the quality of every
article. Of course, the young man answered that
it would; and the Governor added that, while he

was over there in London, he might improve the
opportunity to make acquaintance and establish
correspondence in the bookselling and stationery
business.

Thereupon Gov. Keith urged him to make
ready to set sail. The ship was named the ANNIS,
and the only one at that time making a passage
between Philadelphia and London. It would be
months before she would sail, however; and
Franklin improved the interval, working for Keimer still. He says that during this period he was
fretting about the money he had lent Collins, and
in daily fear lest Vernon should call on him to
pay it over. Keimer and he got along very well
together; Franklin had not yet let him into his
plan of starting the printing business for himself.
They indulged as much in discussion as ever.
Previous to this, and among the earliest of his
studies, Franklin had learned what is styled the
Socratic method of logic, which is by asking questions, instead of committing oneself to any particular view at first, and so winding up one's
opponent with nothing but his own answers. The
chief art of this style of argument lies in starting
a question that appears to have no sort of relation
to the topic under discussion, and leading your

opponent out where he little suspects. The *Socratic method* of arguing was a favorite one with Franklin, from the time in his early youth when he first became acquainted with it until the end of his public career. It may also serve to explain the pointedness of his observations, the terseness of his remarks, and the shrewdness of his reasoning.

The friendship existing between Franklin and Keimer was of a queer texture. Each practised his wit upon the other, and fought as shy in an encounter as two pugilists. Keimer became afraid of Franklin's questions at last, and before answering them, would stop and ask — "what do you mean to infer from that?" He was a free thinker, and proposed to establish a new sect; he was to preach the doctrines, while Franklin was to confound the opponents! Keimer wore his beard of full length, and kept the seventh day of the week for his Sabbath. Franklin was averse to both these points, which, with the other, were essential. So to compromise the matter, Franklin agreed to subscribe to them, if Keimer would give up the use of animal food. The latter thought he could not live without eating meat; but Franklin knew better, and assured him he would be all the healthier for it. He was a great eater, at best, and a change of diet would work an improvement. At last both consented to the proposal, and lived up to it for three months; Franklin confessed that he was as desirous of pleasing himself by half-starving his friend, as anything else. Their provisions were purchased, cooked, and brought to them by a woman in the neighborhood, for whom Franklin made out a list of forty dishes, none of which had parts either of flesh, fish, or fowl. It brought down their living expenses, too, to an exceedingly low figure, eighteen pence sterling per week.

Franklin got on with his new diet famously, for he was somewhat used to it; but Keimer was a great sufferer by the change. Franklin said he "longed for the flesh-pots of Egypt, and ordered a roast pig!" He asked Franklin and a couple of female friends to come and dine off it with him; but as it chanced to be brought a little sooner on the table than he expected, Keimer drew up and ate the whole before the rest came!

Meantime, Franklin was extending his acquaintances. He gives a list of the young men of the town he knew, and mentions particularly that they are *lovers of reading.* "Many pleasant walks we

5*

have had together," says he, in his autobiography, "on Sundays in the woods, on the banks of the Schuylkill, where we read to one another, and conferred on what we had read." One of his young friends was given to writing verses, from which practice a second of the number tried to dissuade him; telling him that if he would succeed in business, he must give his thoughts to nothing but business, and that poetry would only stand in his way. Franklin, too, was not over favorable to the versifying practice, since his father had taken some of his ballad performances in hand for him; he admitted that one might attempt to write verses, but only for the greater command of language which it gave him.

He paid marked attention to Miss Read, at this period, and confesses that he had great respect and affection for her, and good reason to think she entertained the same for him. Possibly they might have married even then, though neither was above eighteen years old; but the girl's mother dissuaded them, saying it would be more proper after his return from England, if at all, than before going; and very likely she wished to see how the young man promised to succeed in his new business. A mother's counsels never come amiss in a matter of this kind.

The names of the four young men who were his closest friends, were Charles Osborne, Joseph Watson, James Ralph, and Charles Brockden. It was Ralph who was given to poetry. Franklin says that Pope finally cured him of being a verse-maker, and he afterwards became a good enough writer of prose. Watson died in his friend Frank-lin's arms, a few years after, "being"—as the latter admits—"the best of our set." Osborne went to the West Indies, where he became emi-nent as a lawyer, accumulated money, and died young. Franklin made an agreement with him, that whichever died first should, if possible, come back and pay a friendly visit to the other, acquaint-ing him with the state of things in the other world; but he adds that "he never fulfilled his promise."

Previous to sailing for England, he was very frequently at the house of the Governor, where the project of the printing office was the prominent topic of their conversation. The governor was lavish with his promises, as usual; he told the youth that he should furnish him with several letters of introduction, beside letters of credit with which to purchase his outfit for the printing office.

Every time these letters were alluded to, Franklin was told to call for them on a future day; and still it was a future day, and seemed likely to be only that.

The ship, too, was delayed, and delayed very much as the foreman put off the performance of his promises; but when the time did come for her to depart, Franklin called at his house to take his leave and get his promised letters. The Governor's secretary, however, even then found an excuse for the Governor, saying that he was very busily engaged writing, and could not attend to him; but he pledged himself that the letters should be aboard the ship at New Castle, to which Franklin immediately repaired. What was his surprise to find the Governor there before him! His Secretary had excused him on the ground of being engaged writing; and now here he was at New Castle! Franklin was not a little puzzled, as he well might be. He was undertaking great things, on a basis that each day looked more and more slender.

He had taken formal leave of Miss Read before joining the ship, and exchanged promises of marriage with her. He also went around among his friends and bade them all farewell. His friend

Ralph embarked at the same time, leaving his wife and child behind; it afterwards came out that he had some difficulty with his wife's relations, and resolved to leave her on their hands altogether. There were several gentlemen of character and respectability on board, who occupied the whole cabin, and compelled Franklin and his friend Ralph to take up with accommodations in the steerage; as nobody knew them, they were not taken special notice of. But Col. French— who was with Gov. Keith when Franklin was invited to the tavern by that gentlemen to taste his Madeira and talk over this very project of going to England, —came on board the ship just before she sailed, and, recognizing the young printer, paid him much attention; the others seeing it, and knowing Col. French to be a personage of official importance in the province of Delaware, at once condescended to take some notice of Franklin themselves; and he and his friend Ralph were both of them invited by the other passengers to take up their quarters in the cabin, one of the gentlemen having concluded to stay behind, thus making room for them.

Franklin asked the Captain of the vessel for the letters from Gov. Keith which were to be under

his care, and which he understood Col. French
had brought on board.   He was informed that all
the letters and dispatches were put into the bag
together, and could not well be got at then; but
he should be allowed to pick them out before
they reached England.   This pacified him in a
degree, and they set sail with favoring winds.
Had Franklin been older, he would never have
undertaken this voyage without so much as
seeing his letters of introduction and of credit, or
even knowing if they were on board; but youth
is both blind and brave.   It would not be deli-
cious youth, if its light feet were shod with the
lead of old men's wisdom.

CHAPTER III.

TO ENGLAND AND BACK.

THE passage to England was marked by no event of special interest. When the ship arrived in the English Channel, the captain gave him leave to look in the bag for his letters, which he proceeded to do, taking out such as concerned him and the business on which he had come. On the day before Christmas, 1724, he arrived in London. On the way across the Atlantic, he had fortunately made the acquaintance of Mr. Denham, an upright and honorable merchant of Philadelphia, whose advice in a period of trouble was of the first importance to him, and who remained his friend so long as he lived.

One of his letters was addressed to the King's Printer, and another to a stationer. He delivered the letter to the stationer first, stating that it was from Gov. Keith. The stationer broke the seal, looked it over, and said, "I don't know such a person;" then, a moment after, he said, "Oh, this is from Riddlesden! I have lately found him to be a complete rascal, and I will have nothing to do with him, nor receive letters from him!" And he gave back the letter into the young man's hand, and turned on his heel. This was a great surprise and disappointment. On looking over the whole affair, Franklin was still more astonished to find that *none* of the letters were from Keith. Under the circumstances, what was he to do,—a youth, a stranger on a strange shore, deceived by a man whose position placed him above the reach even of suspicion in his mind? He bethought himself of Mr. Denham; and to that gentleman he went straightway, and laid before him the whole case. Mr. Denham thereupon exposed Keith's character to young Franklin, without reserve; and told him there was no sort of probability that he had written any letters for him whatever; as for his letters of credit, he had no credit to give, and it made the merchant laugh to think of it. "But," said the young and friendless printer, "what am I to do?" The merchant advised him to think no more of Keith or of his schemes, but to **try** and obtain employment in some London printing office, where he could gain greater skill at his trade, and return to America better prepared than ever to set up in business. It was sound advice, and the young man had the good sense to follow it.

This is the way Franklin himself speaks of this transaction: "What shall we think of a Governor playing such pitiful tricks, and imposing so grossly on a poor ignorant boy! It was a habit he had acquired. He wished to please everybody; and, having little to give, he gave expectations."

He at once took lodgings with his friend Ralph, at three shillings and sixpence a week; and hunted up some poor relations, but they were even poorer than himself! His friend was out of funds, and borrowed of Franklin as long as the latter would or could lend. Franklin got work almost immediately, at Palmer's, a well known printing office of London; and there he remained for almost a year. He says himself he was pretty diligent, yet he spent quite as much money as he ought with Ralph, going to the theatres. The latter soon forgot his wife and child in America, and Franklin began to let Miss

Read pass out of *his* thoughts likewise. That circumstance he counts up as *another* among the decided errors of his life. He never wrote her but one letter, and then only to let her know that he was not likely very soon to return.

In the London printing office, he was put upon a job of setting type for Wollaston's "Religion of Nature." As he got into it, he thought the reasoning faulty, and sat down and wrote a piece himself, criticising the same. He entitled it "A Dissertation on Liberty and Necessity, Pleasure and Pain." This at only nineteen! He had studied Locke and Socrates to some purpose. His employer at once raised his opinion of his youthful apprentice, though he condemned the young man's principles. He printed his own pamphlet, however, and reckoned it as still another of his *errors*. At this time he managed to lay in with a dealer in second-hand books, who permitted him to read and return the books, for a given price. Franklin improved this privilege to the utmost. His pamphlet brought him into acquaintance with a Dr. Lyons, who had written a book on "The Infallibility of Human Judgment." This gentleman paid him great attention; carried him to an alehouse in London

known as " The Horns," and introduced him to
Dr. Mandeville, the author of the " Fable of the
Bees," who was at the head of a club there. At
Batson's Coffee House, Dr. Lyons presented him
to Dr. Pemberton, who promised to take him to
see Sir Isaac Newton; but that privilege he never
enjoyed.

He was invited to a nobleman's house in
Bloomsbury Square, from having brought from
America a purse made of *asbestos*, which fire will
not burn. The nobleman bought it of him to
add to his collection of curiosities, and paid him
a round sum for it. Ralph pretty soon left him,
going into the country to teach a little school,
and taking his friend Franklin's name to establish himself in business with! It was flattering
to young Franklin to know that his name was
worth something to begin upon. Ralph and he
had a falling out at last, about the young woman
with whom the former had been keeping company. He had left her rather under Franklin's
care, and the latter had from time to time
assisted her with small loans in Ralph's absence;
but he having acted improperly to her one day,
she resented his conduct with spirit, wrote to
Ralph about it, and at once brought the school-

master up to London. He expressed himself
very freely to Franklin on his conduct, and said
that now all his obligations to the latter (for
money lent) were discharged. But Franklin
never counted on getting a penny back, the
vagabond having nothing out of which to pay.
This, however, ended their acquaintance.

While in the office, for the sake of getting
needful exercise, he worked at the press,—the
heaviest labor about the establishment. He
thought he was not so well unless he mixed up
this kind of work with his type-setting. He was
a strict water drinker, all the time; while the rest
of the hands, numbering almost fifty, were liberal
consumers of beer. He thought he could lift
more and work harder on water than they could
on their beer. The hands used to call him the
"Water American;" yet they could not fail to
see that he who drank only water was stronger
than they who drank beer.

There was a boy who always brought in the
beer from the neighboring alehouse. The man
who worked at the press with him used to drink,
every day, a pint before breakfast, a pint with his
bread and cheese at breakfast, a pint between
breakfast and dinner, a pint at dinner, a pint

about six o'clock in the afternoon, and a final pint when his day's work was all done! Franklin thought it abominable, and it was. Three quarts of beer every day! The workman thought that *strong* beer, of course, made *him* strong. Franklin sat down to show him how mistaken he was: he demonstrated that the actual strength-giving qualities of beer were in proportion to the amount of barley flour dissolved in the water it is made of; that there was more flour in a penny-worth of bread; and that he would get the most real strength by eating that amount of bread, with nothing but a pint of water, than by drinking down a whole quart of beer. But the man would not be convinced. He kept on drinking his beer, and always had four or five shillings to slice off from his wages every Saturday night, which he might just as well have saved. "And thus," says Franklin, "these poor devils keep themselves always under."

Finally he left the press-room, and was transferred to the composing-room. It was a custom, at that time, for each new comer to pay five shillings to purchase drink for all, and that sum was demanded of Franklin by the workmen; having already paid it to the pressmen, he refused it,

6*

thinking it an imposition, and so thought the master, too. He stood out for two or three weeks; but whenever he came back to his case, after crossing the floor or leaving the room, he was sure to find his "sorts" all mixed up, and other tricks practised freely upon him, which the rest ascribed to the antics of the "chapel ghost," —*chapel* being another name for printing office; and these impositions were followed up so industriously, he finally thought best to give up his resolution and pay what was demanded of him. They told him the "ghost" always haunted those who were not regularly admitted to their number by the payment of the fee, and would probably haunt him till he had paid it. He said he was "convinced of the folly of being on ill terms with those one is to live with continually." From that day forward, he exercised a decided influence over the whole office. He proposed some reasonable alterations in the "chapel's" laws, and succeeded in carrying his point, too.

Many of the men left off drinking beer altogether, from the contagion of his example. They found they could have a large porringer of hot water-gruel for their breakfast, crumbled with bread, spiced with pepper, and a piece of butter

thrown in, for just what they would have to pay
for *a half pint* of beer; they felt better both in
their pockets and heads from the change. The
beer-drinkers, however, were continually obliged
to borrow money through the week; and Franklin used to stand at the pay-table on Saturday
nights, to take up the money from one and another's wages which was due him. Some weeks
he was paid as much as thirty shillings out of
their accounts. His skill as a satirist or *riggite*
made him very popular with them. The master
likewise esteemed him for always being at the
office on Monday; with those who drank beer it
was "Blue Monday,"—or what they also styled
"St. Monday,"—the effect of the Saturday night's
and Sunday's carousals not being yet over. The
master found him so good a hand that he put
him on despatch work, for which he was accus-
tomed to obtain better pay. He changed his
lodgings, too, to a place opposite the Romish
Chapel; the house was kept by a widow lady,
and his room was up three pairs of stairs, back.
She would not take him to lodge until she had
first sent to inquire about him at the place where
he last was; and then she agreed to take him at
the same rate, — cheaper than she otherwise

would, for the sake of having the protection of a male lodger in the house.

The widow was an invalid, and had become a Romanist. Franklin used to go into her room and take supper with her occasionally, enjoying her conversation very greatly. She could tell him stories of what had occurred so far back as the times of Charles the Second. When he talked to her of moving, in order to reduce his expenses and save as much more as he could, she offered to take off two shillings a week rather than lose so good a lodger.

He became acquainted, too, with an eccentric maiden lady who lodged in the house; she was seventy years of age, and lived in the most retired manner possible. She was likewise a Catholic, and tried to lead the life of a nun, up in her high London attic. She gave away to charity all her property, after reserving only twelve pounds a year to subsist on herself; and even out of this meagre sum she still saved something to bestow in charity. She took no nourishment but water-gruel, and had no fire save what was sufficient to boil it. Here she had continued to live for years, none of the occupants of the house disturbing her, but rather preferring to have her stay, as they were

Catholics themselves. Seeing that a priest used to come to confess her, Franklin had the curiosity to ask her how she could find employment for a confessor, living so far out of the reach of sin and temptation. "Oh," replied she, "it is impossible to avoid *vain thoughts!*"

Franklin had been a good swimmer from his early boyhood, and could not be surpassed in the water by any of his companions. He taught a couple of friends to swim from going but twice into the river. These two friends introduced him to some country gentlemen, and they all went to Chelsea by water, to see the College and certain curiosities there. Coming back, the company asked young Franklin to show them how he could perform with his limbs in the river; whereupon he stripped and jumped in, and swam from near Chelsea to Blackfriars, performing various feats by the way, that greatly surprised and delighted them. One of his friends afterwards proposed to travel over Europe together, giving exhibitions and instructions; on asking his good friend Mr. Denham's advice about the matter, he put the young man on the right track again at once, dissuading him from such a project, and urging him to make ready to return very soon with himself to Philadelphia.

Mr. Denham was about to import a large stock of goods, and proposed to Franklin to take him as his clerk,—to keep his books, copy his letters, and take care of his store. That gentleman further promised him that, as soon as he should become familiar with business, he should be sent out with a cargo to the West Indies, bearing commissions from others, which would increase his profits. The young man was altogether pleased with the proposal; he had grown tired of London, and his thoughts reverted to the happy days he had spent in Philadelphia. He agreed with the merchant, therefore, for fifty pounds a year, Pennsylvania money,—which was less than he was then earning, but with a larger prospect. He gave up the printing business, as he thought, forever. Previous to the sailing of the vessel, he went around with Mr. Denham, to observe the operations connected with collecting and packing a stock of goods to be sent beyond the seas.

Just before he left, he received an invitation from a nobleman, Sir William Wyndham, to call and see him; the latter had two sons, who were about starting on their travels, and whom he

wished Franklin to teach the art of swimming,
promising to pay him handsomely. The nobleman had heard of the swimming feat performed
by Franklin, the news having spread rapidly. Had
Franklin been addressed in this way before he had
engaged with Mr. Denham, it is quite probable he
would have closed with the proposal, and remained
in England to teach a swimming-school. But he
came back to America, to deal with *one* of these
sons of Sir William Wyndham,—then become Earl
of Egremont,—in a very different way.

He was in London some eighteen months; he
worked hard all the time, and says he spent very
little upon himself but what it cost him to see
plays and read books. His friend Ralph had
proved a sort of nightmare for him; he owed him
twenty-seven pounds, and this debt kept Franklin
poor all the time. Still he loved the vagabond;
he had known him in other days and places, and
the bond was a strong one. He says he had learned
something by going abroad, and he had read con-
siderably.

The vessel in which he embarked, sailed from
England on the 23d of July, 1726. While at sea,
he deliberately formed a plan for the future conduct of his life; a plan which he r⸱⸱ ⸱ʼᶍ teʼᵥ adhered

to through active manhood and to the close of
an honored old age.   When he reached home, he
found Miss Read married; he would have been
ashamed to meet her but for this strange circumstance : her friends had persuaded her that Franklin would never return, and urged her to marry a
man named Rogers, a potter by trade.

He met Governor Keith on the street, who
seemed ashamed to look at the young printer, and
passed on without speaking ; the Governor had
been deposed in Franklin's absence, and another
put in his place. Keimer, the Philadelphia printer,
had greatly improved his condition, in the mean
time. Mr. Denham opened a store at once on
Water street, and he and his new clerk set to work
displaying their goods. Franklin gave his whole
attention to his employer's business, learned how
to keep accounts and to sell goods, and very soon
became expert in his new calling. He boarded
and lodged with Mr. Denham, who was a father
to him indeed.

Matters went on swimmingly until the following February, when both merchant and clerk were
taken seriously ill—the latter with the pleurisy.
It came near carrying him off; in fact, he says he
had given the world up entirely, and felt not a

little disappointed to find he was recovering! He regretted that he should have "all the disagreeable work to go over again," at some time or another. But though the clerk survived, the employer died. He left Franklin a small token of his love and esteem, and the young man's connection with mercantile business ceased from that day forward.

His brother-in-law, Captain Holmes, happened to be in the city at the time, and advised him to go back to his trade again. Keimer made him an offer of good wages by the year, to come and take the management of his printing office, and, after much hesitation, he took up with it. He had heard bad stories of this man's character from his wife's relatives, while in London, and he hesitated for that reason. But nothing better promised, and he took what he could get first. The office was full of raw hands, and Franklin soon saw that Keimer's object in offering him large wages was a purely selfish one: he would have the London workman teach these poorer tradesmen, and then turn him off to shift for himself. But he made no needless complaint; he went about setting the office in order and getting the workmen in the most serviceable condition. Among the printers in the office was an Oxford scholar.

7

He got on very comfortably with the hands, for they respected him for his skill and were glad to learn of him. He says that, as Keimer did not work on Saturday, that being his Sabbath, he had "two days for reading." He was contented and happy; nothing gave him uneasiness but the money of Vernon's which he had long ago collected and lent to Collins. His ingenuity was a real source of profit to the establishment; for when the office needed types and engravings of a certain kind, and even ink, Franklin went to work and *manufactured* them. He says himself that he was "quite a *factotum*." But things soon began to betray a change: the more skilful the workmen under him became, the less need Keimer had of his services; and so the employer searched for pretexts on which to base a feeling of dissatisfaction, and finally a quarrel. On paying Franklin his second quarter's wages, Keimer told him that they were *too much*, and thought he should take off a part from them. From that time he behaved uncivilly, and pretty soon with undisguised impertinence and hostility. Franklin, however, bore all with exemplary patience.

But, one day, Keimer looked up at the upper window of the office from the street, where a hub-

bub of some sort had taken place, and chanced
to spy Franklin with his head out to see what was
the matter. It was the occasion he wanted. The
irritated employer bawled out to Franklin, in a
loud and angry tone, to take his head in and mind
his business; and coupled his order with some
abusive words that could not but offend the
young printer exceedingly; all the neighbors
heard it, and that only served to make the matter
worse. Soon after, Keimer came up-stairs, and
continued his violent and abusive language.
High words were given on both sides. Keimer
was sorry he was obliged to give Franklin a
quarter's notice, before he could get rid of him.
Franklin replied that he would not hold him to
that, but was ready to be quit of him even then:
and he did take his hat, and walk straight out
of doors, telling one of the workmen, named
Meredith, to pick up what belonged to him and
bring them round that evening to his room.

When Meredith entered his apartment at night,
he found Franklin seriously thinking about returning to Boston, and dissuaded him from it.
He assured the latter that Keimer was already in
debt for all the stock in the office and store, that
his creditors were beginning to be uneasy; that

he kept his shop but poorly, sold for ready money
without making a profit, kept loose accounts of
his businsss, and would soon have to fail, at any
rate; then there would be a good chance for another man to step into the business.   Besides,
Meredith reminded him that his own time with
Keimer would be out in the spring, and proposed
to him to set up business then together : he to
furnish the *stock* and Franklin the *skill*, in the co-
partnership, and the profits to be shared equally.
Franklin accepted a proposal that promised so
fairly.   Meredith's father also approved of it,
especially as he rejoiced at Franklin's influence
over his son in curing him of the habit of dram-
drinking.

Franklin made out a list of things which would
be wanted in the new office, and handed it to
Meredith's father.   They were to be sent for to
London, and all was to be kept secret until they
should arrive; meantime, our young printer
friend was to try and subsist by obtaining work
at his trade.   He applied to the other printing-
office, but could get nothing there; and so he
remained idle, and was likely to be, until the
stock should come over from England.   But
Keimer chanced to have a prospect of a job of

printing some paper-money for New Jersey, requiring cuts and various types such as only Franklin could supply; and as he was afraid that his rival, Bradford, would now employ Franklin and get the job away from him, he sent the latter a very proper message to come and work for him again, adding that old friends should not part for a few words. Meredith advised his taking up with the offer, and he did. Matters went on then more pleasantly than ever. Keimer got the New Jersey job, and Franklin made a copperplate press to do it with,—the first, he says, that had been seen in this country. He also cut several ornaments and checks for the bills. Then he went over with Keimer to Burlington, and both executed the work there to the satisfaction of the authorities. Keimer received a large amount of money for the job, and was thus saved from going overboard in business.

Young Franklin made a good many valued friends while he stayed in Burlington, including several of the first men in the place. One of them, an elderly man and the surveyor-general of the province, told him confidentially that he (Franklin) would supplant his employer in due time, and set up in business for himself in Phila-

7*

delphia, where he would be sure to make his fortune. He little knew that the young man had just that plan in mind at the time.

Franklin discovered, too, while there, that his employer was jealous of him, because of his superior attainments and the attention they naturally attracted from others. The young printer had been a constant reader, and therefore had a better stored and better disciplined mind than his employer. In fact, it is to this that he ascribes the partiality which was shown him on that occasion, and often afterwards. Of Keimer he says that "he was an odd creature, ignorant of common life, fond of rudely opposing received opinions, slovenly to extreme dirtiness, enthusiastic in some points of religion, and a little knavish withal."

Three months were thus passed in Burlington, during which time he made all possible improvement in every way. In his account of himself along through this period, he speaks very plainly of the loose habits of thinking, on religious topics especially, into which he had fallen. He says that he began to doubt of revelation itself. A work against Deism fell into his hands; but its perusal wrought just an opposite effect from the one to be expected. The arguments which were quoted merely to be answered, made a deeper impression on his mind than the refutations; and he soon became, in fact, a confirmed Deist.

His sober reflections, however, tended to correct these opinions afterwards. He confessed that this doctrine, though it might be true, was not very useful. He felt sincere regrets for having written and published the pamphlet he did in London, with the motto "Whatever is, is right." It did not look to him now like so clever a performance as he once thought it. He says that, about this time, he became convinced that "*truth, sincerity, and integrity,*" were of the utmost importance in dealings between man and man, as well as in the happiness of life; and he formed "written resolutions," to practice them so long as he lived. He confessed that Revelation had no weight with him merely as such; yet he cherished an opinion that, "though certain actions might not be bad *because* they were forbidden by it, or good *because* it commanded them, yet, probably, those actions might be forbidden *because* they were bad for us, or commanded *because* they were beneficial to us."

He acknowledges that he was carried safely

through the temptations of youth by "the kind
hand of Providence or some guardian angel;"
and he felt grateful that it was so. Away from
the restraints of home and friends, thrown among
persons and scenes to which he was unaccus-
tomed, he had reason afterwards to rejoice that
he preserved even "a tolerable character to begin
the world with," and determined to preserve and
make the best possible use of it.

CHAPTER IV.

IN BUSINESS.

THE new fonts of type came from London soon after Franklin returned to Philadelphia. He and his partner had fortunately settled up all their business with Keimer before their arrival, so that the latter had not so much as heard of the movement before it was all ready to be set on foot. In those days, when there was but one, or at most but two printing offices in a town of the size of Philadelphia, such an event would very soon become public, and of course excite more or less talk and commotion. It would be no such an event now, even in any one of the many thriving villages of the country.

The new firm rented a house near the Philadelphia Market, at twenty-four pounds a year; but in order to reduce the rent, they let in a glazier and his family, who were to pay a good share of it to the young printers, while the latter

boarded with them. It was a thrifty way of getting along. Their first customer, as job printers,
was a man from the country whom a good friend
brought into their work-room. As all their cash
had been laid out in procuring what was necessary for the office, they were very glad to take
the five-shilling job which the stranger brought
them. Franklin says that those shillings gave
him more pleasure than "any *crown*" he ever
received afterwards; and he felt such strong
gratitude for the friend who had put this first
piece of work in his hands, that he believes it
had the effect ever after to make him willing to
aid young beginners.

One day he was met by a *croaker*. There are
such men everywhere; they infest every community, and make it their chief business to throw
wet blankets over whatever undertakings come
to their ears. This person was named Samuel
Mickle: he was an elderly man, and an utter
stranger to Franklin; but he took the liberty to
stop him one day at his door, and ask him "if he
was the young man who had lately opened a new
printing-house." He said he was very sorry to
find the report true, for the undertaking was
great, and the cost of it would all be thrown

away. He likewise told young Franklin that Philadelphia was "a sinking place," the people were already "half bankrupts," and the new buildings going up were but deceitful promises of prosperity, and were certain in time to ruin them. The effect produced on the youthful printer's mind by this lugubrious kind of talk was to leave it in a half melancholy state; in fact, he declared that if he had met with this man before embarking in business for himself, he never should have made the venture.

But Franklin records as a fact worth laying up against this man, and all the other men of his class, that he continued to live in Philadelphia notwithstanding the decay into which the city was falling, and kept up his croaking as briskly as ever. He refused for a long time to buy a house there, because he was so sure the place was rapidly going to ruin; and Franklin remarks that it gave him "pleasure" to see him at last obliged to give five times as much for a house as he would have had to do, had he bought when he first began croaking!

About this time, Franklin set in operation a club of young men, who were to meet for self-improvement, which club was named the JUNTO.

They met on Friday evenings. The rules required that each member should in turn bring in a question to be discussed in open meeting, on any point of morals, politics, or natural philosophy; and once in three months he was to read before the body an essay of his own production, on any subject whatever. There was a President appointed by the club, and it was agreed that all debates and discussions should be carried on in a sincere spirit of inquiry after truth, and not merely from a vain desire for victory. If a member used improper language, or was hasty, or indulged in open contradiction of others, he was to be fined in a small sum of money.

The members of this Junto were not altogether indifferent characters. It was not exactly a club to count among its members such men as Sir Joshua Reynolds, Edmund Burke, Oliver Goldsmith, and Dr. Samuel Johnson,— but it was made immortal by at least one spirit within its little circle, and that one Benjamin Franklin. There was a copier of deeds among them, the inventor of Hadley's Quadrant, a professional surveyor, a shoemaker, a joiner, a young gentleman of some fortune who was given to *punning*, and, finally, the clerk of a merchant, William

Coleman by name, who had, as Franklin himself records it, "the coolest, clearest head, the best heart, and the exactest morals" of any man he ever met with.

This same merchant's clerk afterwards became a great merchant, and one of the judges of the province. He and Franklin continued fast friends for the term of forty years, for almost the whole of which time the club likewise continued; and Franklin says it was "the best school of philosophy, morality, and politics, that then existed in the province." In order to discuss the various topics with anything like justice, it of course became necessary for the members to read carefully beforehand such works as treated of the matter under consideration; and the rules required such carefulness in speaking, and forbade with such strictness all indulgence in intemperate and improper language, that the young men soon found they were receiving such real benefit from the weekly meetings as they had scarcely deemed possible. There was no temper lost between them, which only left so much more room and time for personal improvement.

This same Club brought the new printing-house *business*. The several members of it made

8

it a point to influence all they could in favor of
the young printers. Through one they procured
the printing of forty sheets of the new Quaker
history; Keimer performed the rest of the work,
and Franklin said they took their part on such
low terms as scarcely allowed a profit. They
worked hard over the job, Franklin himself composing a sheet each day, and frequently not
finishing his day's work till eleven o'clock at
night.

He was so eager to make his sheet a day, that
one night, after having placed his "forms" on
the "imposing stone," he accidentally made "pi"
of two pages; all of which he deliberately went
to work and set in type again before he went to
bed. By industry of this sort, closely followed
up, the new house soon acquired reputation and
earned the confidence of all who knew or heard
of its partners. Although it was continually
thrown out at the Merchants' Club that the new
printing-house was sure to fail, there being two
similar houses in town already, yet the young
men held steadily on their way. One gentleman,
a friend of theirs, predicted differently, however:
he said — "the industry of that Franklin is
superior to anything of the kind I ever saw; I

see him at work when I go home from the club, and he is at work again before his neighbors are out of bed." The remark was not without its effect in the young men's favor.

Franklin confesses that it was this homely virtue of industry that brought the concern up, and afterwards kept it there. He wished his posterity to know and remember how much is due to the exercise of that single virtue.

It was not long before it entered into the plans of Franklin to publish a newspaper in Philadelphia, in connection with his job business. He had had some experience in that line in Boston, as the reader will remember; and he felt confident of his ability to go forward with a plan which would add to his own personal influence as well as increase the profits of his establishment. An old fellow printer at Keimer's had purchased his time of his employer, and came over to Franklin's office to offer himself as a journeyman. As it happened, they had no work just then to give him; but Franklin told him in confidence that he should start a newspaper soon, and that he would probably have work for him then.

The only newspaper printed in the city was by Bradford, and a wretched affair it was.

Yet it paid him a good profit, and Franklin reasoned that if an affair of that kind paid well, a better one ought to pay better; and he determined to try the experiment. But Webb was leaky; he could not keep his important secret, but must needs tell it to Keimer. Upon the hint thus received, Keimer resolved to begin a new paper himself, before Franklin should get ready for his enterprise. He would thus have the field all to himself. Franklin was not a little chagrined at the occurrence, and quite as much vexed; and in order to do all the damage possible to Keimer's prospects, he sat down and wrote a number of pleasant pieces for Bradford's paper,—the very one he had determined to overthrow, — over the signature of Busy Body. These articles were kept up by him for several months, and attracted special attention. Everything relating to Keimer's paper, his proposals to the public not excepted, were ridiculed to the last letter.

Keimer started his paper, however, according to his proposals; but he had not gone on with it fully nine months, during which period he had not more than ninety subscribers at any one time, when he turned and offered the whole concern to

Franklin for a mere song. The latter had been all ready for the step for some little time, and of course fell in with his proposal without further delay. It became very profitable to him in a few years. His partner, Meredith, became worse than helpless in the establishment; for in addition to being a wretched compositor and pressman he was seldom sober. A favorable opportunity for dissolving the business relations not long afterwards occurred.

Franklin put his best care and talent into the columns of his newspaper; he believed, too, as any practical printer would, that an attractive mechanical appearance made a great difference in favor of any paper; therefore he took exceeding pains with the types and the printing. A dispute, since become historical, which was then going on between the Governor and the Massachusetts Assembly, led him to make pointed remarks on the same from time to time, which drew still wider attention to his paper, and soon made the principal people his subscribers. When a few leading men began to take the paper, their example was followed very soon and very generally. Franklin sets down all his good luck at this critical period as the result of "having learned a little to scribble." And, on the other hand, the man who could himself

8*

"handle a pen" in conducting a newspaper, was thought twice as well of as if he could not. Hence he was encouraged in every manner.

Bradford, his rival, had printed an address of the House to the Governor in such a careless and blundering manner, Franklin resolved to improve upon it and watch the effect. So he reprinted the whole in a style of elegance and with all attention to correctness, and sent a copy to each member of the House. The entire body saw the difference in the style of the work, and the friends of Franklin were thus enabled to command votes enough to make him and his partner public printers for the following year.

Meredith's father, who had engaged to advance the money for the printing office, and who had advanced but one hundred pounds already, was unable to make the *second* payment of an hundred pounds, as expected. In consequence, the firm was sued for the amount; bail was given; but it was plain to Franklin that, when the case came to trial, judgment would be given against them, execution would follow, and every vestige of their industry and their hopes would vanish. In this dilemma he was waited upon by a couple of true friends, each ignorant of what the other had done,

who offered him the help he so much needed in
order to take the whole business on his own shoulders. They did not wish him to continue the
connection with Meredith, however, who had repeatedly been seen drunk in the streets, and whose
haunts were low ale-houses.

The names of these two men who so generously
offered him this timely assistance were William
Coleman and Robert Grace. He thanked each
of them from his heart; but he felt obliged to tell
them that he was not at liberty to break up the
partnership so long as there remained any chance
of Meredith's father keeping his engagement in
the matter of the second payment. Yet if he
should fail entirely to do so, then their proffered
aid would be most gladly accepted.

Not long after, Franklin held a talk with his
partner about the business, and asked him if he
thought his father declined to advance more money on account of being dissatisfied with himself.
The young man positively assured him that that
was not the reason at all; "my father has been
disappointed," said he, "and is really unable, and
I am unwilling to distress him further." His
partner likewise told him that he felt certain that
he was unfit for the business, and ought to give

it up. He was Welsh; many of his people were about to colonize and emigrate to North Carolina; and he felt inclined to leave with them and go upon the land again to work. He had been bred a farmer, and not a printer; land was very cheap where they talked of going, and he was certain to get at least a living there, if he did not do more. He also made Franklin a proposition to assume the debts of the firm, to pay back the hundred pounds the elder Meredith had advanced, clear off his personal debts, give him thirty pounds and a new saddle,—and the whole concern should be turned over to his hands.

Franklin lost no time in acceding to this proposal. He had it duly drawn up in writing, signed, and sealed. Payments were made as proposed, and his partner left him for the distant province of North Carolina. He wrote back a couple of letters from that country the next year, filled with sensible and reliable accounts of the climate, soil, and productions, which Franklin published in the columns of his paper.

Rather than seem partial to either of his two kind friends, he wisely accepted half of what each had offered him, and at once paid off the company debts, and went on with the business. He made a public announcement in his paper that the partnership was dissolved.

A lively discussion concerning paper money sprang up at this time. There were but £15,000 of it in the province, and this was soon to be funded. One class of the people opposed the plan of increasing the amount in circulation, believing that it would become so plentiful as to grow too cheap, requiring a large amount to buy the same articles. This same question had come up for discussion in the Junto, and Franklin had there advocated an addition to the paper currency; he said he was persuaded, from the small amount which was first struck off, in 1723, that it had increased trade, multiplied employments, and brought more population into the province; he now saw all the old houses occupied, and many new ones going up; whereas, when he first strolled about the streets of Philadelphia, munching his roll, he noticed on many and many a house a bill reading —*To be Let*, which led him to think the inhabitants might be deserting the city.

He wrote and published a pamphlet on the subject of paper money, entitled—"*The Nature and Necessity of a Paper Currency.*" The mass of the people received it with favor, but the wealthy class

disliked it, as it swelled the cry for more pape
money. But the production was not answered by
any writer on their side, and the House passed a
bill for printing more paper currency by a decided
majority. Very naturally, as Franklin had taken
such an interest in the measure, and had done so
much toward creating a public opinion for it, the
House voted him the profitable job of doing the
printing. It was another advance in his fortunes,
and he ascribed it all to his having qualified himself early to express his views in writing.

He also obtained the job of printing the same
sort of money for Newcastle, through the inter-
ventions of a friend; and, in addition to that, the
printing of the laws and votes of the same government, which he continued to do as long as he
followed the printing business.

Besides the printing office and the newspaper,
he now opened a stationer's shop, in which he
kept the most correct blanks that had ever made
their appearance among the people. He likewise
kept for sale paper, parchment, chapmen's books,
and other things of the same character. He had
so much work and business on his hands at this
time, that he hired another hand at the case, besides taking in an apprentice. Under the im-

proved state of circumstances in which he found himself, he began to pay off his printing-house debt.

He said that he took a great deal of pains not only to *be* frugal and industrious, but not to appear the contrary; thus paying proper regard to the eyes and opinions of others. He dressed very plain, and never allowed himself to be seen at places of public amusement. He never went off fishing or shooting. He sometimes allowed himself the luxury of reading a *book*, but that did not occur too often, and caused no remark by others. To let people see that he was not above his business, he sometimes wheeled home the paper he bought at the store on a wheelbarrow. Seeing what his character was, merchants went out of their way to solicit his trade, offering to sell him anything he needed in the line of his business on most accommodating terms. He prospered rapidly; while his rival, Keimer, saw his business and his credit fast melting away, and was finally forced to sell his printing-house in order to satisfy his creditors. The man set sail for Barbadoes, where he lived very poor.

An apprentice of Keimer's, whom Franklin had himself instructed when he worked in the office of the former, bought his printing materials and set up in opposition to Franklin, and the latter had some fears lest he would find in him a powerful rival; out of prudence, therefore, he proposed a partnership with him; but it was rejected in a very scornful way, as he was above the reach of such working mechanics as young Franklin. The latter had reason, however, to be grateful for the refusal; for the fellow was vain and conceited, dressed above his situation, did not follow his business, lived showily, ran in debt, and wasted a great deal of time in amusements. His business very soon ran out, and he followed his old master out to Barbadoes, where the apprentice had the satisfaction of hiring his former employer as a journeyman.

Bradford was now the only other printer in Philadelphia. But he was become rich in his business, and did not need to push rivalry with a young man to the limit to which other men would. He was the post-master, however, and as he possessed many facilities for distributing his newspaper which Franklin did not, he obtained more advertisements on the strength of it. In order to get his paper sent by the post, Franklin was forced to bribe the riders, who carried them without

Bradford's knowledge; the latter having expressly forbidden them to take any copies of the rival paper. Franklin has put it on record, to be remembered by all honorable men forever, that when he afterwards came to occupy Bradford's position as post-master, he took special care not to imitate so very mean a practice.

Godfrey and his family had occupied a part of his house all this time, and Franklin had boarded with them. One side of the shop was occupied by Godfrey for his avocation—that of a glazier. Mrs. Godfrey had a relative, who had a daughter; and the kind woman, seeing that the young printer was prospering so well, and feeling more or less interested in his personal welfare, set her wits to work making a match. She brought them together in her apartments as often as possible, and he admits that, on his own side, a serious courtship actually ensued. The girl's father and mother, too, not to be behindhand, took pains to ask him to their house to tea, from time to time, and adroitly left them in one another's company so often that he found it soon became necessary to explain. Here the ready Mrs. Godfrey came in again with her diplomacy. She expected to see the fruits of her tact and skill forthwith.

9

On his part, Franklin wanted her to make the parents of the girl understand that, if he married her, he should expect with her, by way of dowry, as much money as would suffice to pay off the remaining debts of his printing establishment,— perhaps a hundred pounds. Word was brought back by her that they had no such sum to spare. He suggested that they mortgage their house for the purpose in the loan office. They retorted that they did not approve the match; because, having made inquiry of Bradford (his rival), he had told them the printing business was very risky in the province, and that two men had but recently been compelled to give it up—Keimer and his apprentice. Bradford told them, too, that types soon wore out, and would have to be replaced at the same expense as at first. Franklin was therefore forbidden the house, and his lady-love was duly shut up where he could not see her. He doubted if the parents really meant to carry out this resolution, or if it were not part of a plan to draw him into marrying their daughter stealthily, or against their will.

He suspected this plan just strongly enough to suffer his feelings to be touched with resentment, and that concluded his attentions in that quarter.

Mrs. Godfrey afterwards reported to him that the father and mother felt better inclined toward him, and would have been glad to bring about an arrangement; but he held out against any such thing, and at length felt compelled to tell her plainly that he would have nothing more to do with the family. She resented it as a personal matter; and the result was, the Godfreys soon formed a resolution to leave his premises. This left him quite alone in the house; and he made up his mind to take no more inmates.

It was a fortunate occurrence for him, however, and it would seem as if it could have taken place at no more fit period in his whole career. By being thus left alone, and feeling still more so in consequence of being suddenly denied that female society to which he was naturally drawn, his attention was attracted to marriage in earnest. He says he "looked around" him, and "made overtures of acquaintance in other places;" but as it was the prevailing opinion that a printer's business was but a poor one at best, he saw pretty clearly that he could not obtain a wife with money, unless he would consent to take up with just such an one as he did not want.

As it fell out, too, this time in his favor again,

a friendly acquaintance was about this time renewed
between himself and the Read family, who had
all of them kept alive a kind regard for Franklin
since he first went to their house to lodge. They
now called him in quite often to consult in their
private matters, and he proved serviceable to them.
Of course he was obliged to come in contact with
Miss Read,—who, the reader will remember, had
married since Franklin broke off the acquaintance
while in London, and afterwards been deserted
by her husband. She appeared sad and shy to
him, speaking but little, and seeming to dislike
company.

His pity was awakened for her at once. He
accused himself with being the author of all her
mistakes and sorrows, from having neglected her
so cruelly while absent in London; although the
mother of the young woman was by no means of
the same opinion, charging the fault upon herself
for not consenting to their marriage *before* he went
to London, as he had desired. Besides, it was
through her means that the other, and worthless,
match was brought about in Franklin's absence.
The affection was speedily revived between them,
and marriage was very naturally thought of by
both.

But here an ugly obstacle interposed. It was, to be sure, believed that her husband had a wife living in England, which would of course render the former marriage invalid; but the difficulty was, to prove it. There was a story of his death, too; but that could not be proved, either, and to sum up with, he had left many debts behind, which the next husband would legally be called on to pay.

Franklin says he got bravely over all these difficulties, however, and at last married her. The wedding day was on the 1st of September, 1730, and he was a little more than twenty-four and a half years old. It so happened that he was never troubled with any of those inconveniences from which he had feared, and life began pleasantly again with them both.

At that time, there was not a good bookstore, or bookseller's shop, as they then styled them, to the south of Boston. The printers in New York and Philadelphia were stationers, but they sold nothing more than "paper, almanacs, ballads, and a few common school-books." Whoever wanted books, must needs send out to England and import them. We can now hardly imagine the state of things in this country which existed then.

9*

The members of the Junto each had a few books. They had left the alehouse where they held their first meetings, and hired a room elsewhere. Franklin proposed that they should club their books together, and thus make a respectable library, placing them in the club-room. There each member could consult all the books, or carry away for the time such as he would like to read at home. The proposal was at once accepted by the rest as a sensible one, and marked improvement grew out of it.

The success of this new plan of his led him to attempt larger things. Though the members of the club took their books back home after the expiration of a twelvemonth, owing to the trouble found in taking the proper care of them and keeping them safely together, the experience gained by the working of the new plan encouraged Franklin to set on foot a subscription for a large Public Library, to be held for the common benefit of the subscribers to the fund.

He engaged Mr. Charles Brockden, a well-known scrivener and conveyancer of Philadelphia, to draw up articles of agreement to be subscribed; according to which, every subscriber was to pay a certain sum down for the first purchase of the books, and an annual amount to buy more with. Readers were a scanty part of society in Philadelphia at that time; with all his efforts, Franklin could raise but fifty persons, and they chiefly young tradesmen, who were willing to pay down forty shillings apiece, besides an assessment of ten dollars per annum.

But the undertaking was launched with this amount, and faith and industry supplied all deficiencies. They imported their books, and on a given day each week the library was opened to subscribers. The latter gave written notes to pay double the value of the books they took out, unless duly returned.

By and by, similar associations sprang up elsewhere,—not only in other towns, but in the other provinces. It became fashionable to read books; and fashion often works more effectually than sense or reason. The people generally became better acquainted with books. Those who had volumes of their own to contribute, generously gave them to the library; so that it became more and more respectable for the number of its volumes. The result of the increased reading of the citizens of Philadelphia soon made itself visible; people from other places remarked that they appeared better instructed and more intelligent than men of the same class in other communities.

Franklin never forgot one remark made by Mr. Brockden, when the subscribers to the enterprise were about to sign their names to the articles drafted by him. These articles were to be binding on all of them for the term of fifty years. Said Mr. Brockden—"You are young men; but it is scarcely probable that any of you will live to see the expiration of the term fixed in the instrument." Many of them did live over the term of time alluded to, although their company changed the character of its organization by securing a regular charter, which gave it corporate form and legal existence.

One little reflection, put forth by Franklin himself, is at this point worth heeding by young persons. He observed that a good plan was often injured by its author's going about personally and thrusting it on the attention of others, when by keeping himself a little more out of sight it would be sure of speedy success. Therefore he laid it down as a rule for himself, at this period of his life, to operate his schemes as much as possible through others, instead of exhibiting himself;

and he found that it worked to a charm. He left his testimony that the present sacrifice of vanity would always be well repaid by the substantial results that are certain to follow.

CHAPTER V.

GETTING ALONG.

IN the new library he found not only a ready solace from the cares and labors of his business, but likewise a means of improvement of which he was prompt to avail himself. He resolved now to pursue a fixed course of reading and study, for which he set apart at least one or two hours each day. In the course of time, this habit would not fail to produce its peculiar effect on his mind and character.

Here and now did Benjamin Franklin, while he was daily hard at work at his printing case and printing press, industriously build upon the foundations so hastily laid while he was an apprentice in Boston. He says he did what he could to repair the loss of the learned education his father had once intended for him. All the recreation he allowed himself was reading. He wasted no time in games, frolics, or taverns; and he continued working at his trade with all the energy he had at command.

In fact, it was a rather hard row he had to hoe, at best; he was in debt for his printing office; he had a young family; there were two business rivals who had started before him in Philadelphia; and there was need that every hour should be profitably employed. But he felt much encouraged, too, at finding that his business was growing better, and his circumstances easier in consequence. He continued just as frugal as ever, keeping constantly in mind that proverb of Solomon which his father had often repeated to him while a boy,—"Seest thou a man diligent in his calling? He shall stand before Kings; he shall not stand before mean men."

Little thought he, while revolving this same proverb in his mind, that it would be by reason of his *diligence*, as well as of his other virtues, that he would in truth "stand before Kings." But from the time when he began to see that his prosperity was the result of his diligence, he had faith to believe that industry was at the bottom of all success in life. He admits that he did not expect to "stand before Kings," although he did afterwards have the honor to stand before *five*, and to sit down to eat with one,—the King of Denmark. A much more enviable distinction in that day than in this; yet it is well worth noticing on account of the literal fulfillment, in his case, of the proverb.

He speaks himself of his own and his wife's *thrift* at this time, to show the direct results of frugality. He always consulted *his wife* in his undertakings, obeying another proverb, but an old English one, that says,—"He that would thrive, must ask his wife." He sets it down in his autobiography as a piece of singular fortune, that he had a wife who was just as saving and industrious as himself. She took hold with all possible cheerfulness, and helped him in his business; folding and stitching pamphlets, buying old linen rags (that was before the days of cotton) for the papermakers, and tending shop just as he would have done himself.

To show how prudently they lived,—they kept no servants about them to be idle; their table was set with none but plain and simple food; and their furniture was as cheap as possible. For a long while, he ate for his breakfast nothing more than bread and milk, using no tea; and this frugal meal he took from an earthen porringer which cost him only two pennies, with a pewter spoon! This was the style in which a philosopher set up housekeeping with his wife,—a man who was yet to represent his country abroad, and to "stand before kings."

He soon after had occasion, however, to lament the ill effects of prosperity, for it tempted luxury to come into his dwelling. He says that he was greatly surprised, one morning, on being called to breakfast, to find that *a china bowl* was set before him, with *a silver spoon* in it. He knew nothing of it beforehand, his faithful wife being resolved to greet him with a new pleasure. He states that this present cost her "the enormous sum of three and twenty shillings." The only excuse she plead for such an act of extravagance was, that she thought *her* husband was as deserving of a china bowl and silver spoon as any of his neighbors. This was the first piece of china and the first piece of plate introduced into his family. They had a great deal of it afterwards.

His religious views and feelings now claimed a large share of his attention. He felt it to be necessary to take a serious review of his life and character, and endeavor to shape his conduct so as to challenge the closest scrutiny of his own

10

conscience, and merit the approbation of his
Maker. Though he had been educated in the
tenets of the Presbyterians, he thought some of
their points of faith unintelligible, and others
doubtful; and he therefore declined to attend on
public worship, making of Sunday what he called
his "studying day." He confesses that he was
never without religious principles. He did not,
for example, question the existence of God; or
that He created and governs the world; or that
the most acceptable service of God was the doing
good to man; or that the soul is immortal; or
that all crime will be punished, and all virtue
will be rewarded, either here or hereafter.

These points he believed to be the very essen-
tials of religion; and he respected all creeds, in
proportion to the infusion which they had of
these very principles. And hence, respecting all
creeds, and not being unwilling to believe that
"even the worst had some good effects," he carefully avoided all discourse that might incline a
person to think less of his own religion. Besides
this example of his toleration, he contributed
something to every sect that had it in mind to
erect a new place of public worship, never refusing their solicitations. And during the whole

time that he declined attending church, he still paid in his annual subscription to the only Presbyterian minister or meeting they had in Philadelphia.

The minister used to come and visit Franklin, and admonish him of his duty to attend on his preaching, and he admits that he was prevailed to do so, from time to time: once for five Sundays together. He says he would have gone to hear him preach regularly, but for the fact that he preached discourses that were filled with polemic arguments, or matters of creed, which to his mind seemed "dry, uninteresting, and unedifying." He thought such sermons calculated to make good *Presbyterians*, rather than good *citizens*. And therefore he stayed away, and pursued his Sunday course of studies.

But Franklin speaks of one sermon in particular, which he thought ought certainly to prove a test of the value of his preaching, so far as *he* was to be benefited. The text was from Philippians, reading thus:—"Finally, brethren, whatsoever things are true, honest, just, pure, lovely, or of good report, if there be any virtue or any praise, think on these things." Franklin thought that, from a text of this sort, the preacher could not easily go wide of a practical discourse on morals and morality. Instead of that, he proceeded to lay down five points, as follows: 1st. Keeping holy the Sabbath day. 2d. Being diligent in reading the holy Scriptures. 3d. Attending duly the public worship. 4th. Partaking of the Sacrament. 5th. Paying a due respect to God's ministers. Franklin thought himself that all these might be good things, but they were not the kind of good things to be expected from that text; and, despairing of getting what he craved from any other text if not from that, he confesses that he was "disgusted, and attended his preaching no more."

His mind, however, was profoundly exercised about moral improvement. He aimed to have his head and heart grow in wisdom and purity together. It seems that, a few years before, he had sat down and composed for his own private use a form of prayer, or liturgy, which he had entitled—"Articles of Belief and Acts of Religion;" and he went back to the regular and conscientious use of this little composition, declining to attend upon public worship any more. He does not attempt to excuse his conduct in this respect, leaving results to speak for him.

Along with the discipline obtained by this course, he was led to conceive a project of actually reaching a state of "moral perfection;" a bold enterprise for a young man, but one in which a trial would lead him to at least a better understanding of himself than he ever possessed before. He says that he wished "to live without committing any fault at any time, and to conquer all that either natural inclination, custom, or company might lead him into." He thought, that, since he knew what was right and what was wrong, there would be no difficulty in always doing the one and avoiding the other. But he little understood the character or extent of the task he had undertaken. He could no more than give his attention to one fault, in order to correct and remove it, when he found that he had committed a fault in another direction! To use his own phrase concerning the matter,—"habit took the advantage of inattention, and inclination was sometimes too strong for reason."

His many slips had the effect, however, to open his eyes to what he would not so soon have discovered in any other way; he became wise in a direction where he might long have been in darkness, but for this faulty experiment: and he at

10*

last came to the conclusion that no person could become completely virtuous from the conviction that it was for his interest to become so, and that all opposite habits must be broken, and really good ones established in their places, before one can rely on a steady rectitude of conduct.

In order to bring about, in his own case, the establishment of thoroughly good habits in place of the contrary, he resorted to a method original with himself, extremely ingenious while likewise simple, and one which deserves the closest examination, if not the most conscientious imitation, of all young men of like desires and aspirations. He sat down and made a *catalogue* of all the leading virtues he had ever met with in the course of his reading, enumerating *thirteen* in all, and affixing to each a short precept which illustrated its meaning. They are all given here, in their order, for the sake of more clearly showing the nature and extent of the task which he had resolutely set before him:

1. TEMPERANCE.—Eat not to dulness; drink not to elevation.

2. SILENCE.—Speak not but what may benefit others or yourself; avoid trifling conversation.

3. ORDER.—Let all things have their places; let each part of your business have its time.

4. RESOLUTION.—Resolve to perform what you ought; perform without fail what you resolve.

5. FRUGALITY.—Make no expense but to do good to others or yourself; that is, waste nothing.

6. INDUSTRY.—Lose no time; be always employed in something useful; cut off all unnecessary actions.

7. SINCERITY.—Use no hurtful deceit; think innocently and justly; and, if you speak, speak accordingly.

8. JUSTICE.—Wrong none by doing injuries, or omitting the benefits that are your duty.

9. MODERATION.—Avoid extremes; forbear resenting injuries so much as you think they deserve.

10. CLEANLINESS.—Tolerate no uncleanliness in body, clothes, or habitation.

11. TRANQUILLITY.—Be not disturbed at trifles, or at accidents common or unavoidable.

12. CHASTITY. — — — — —

13. HUMILITY.—Imitate Jesus and Socrates.

His object was to form habits, or, as he ex-

presses it, "to acquire habitudes," of virtue; and
he conceived a plan by which he thought he could
make more headway than by any other.

He determined to rivet his attention on *one of
these virtues* at a time, rather than attempt to compass them all at once, and thus lose the impression of all.   After mastering *one* of them, he
would go on to another; and thus pass through
the whole catalogue.   And he reasoned again,
that his conscientious practice of one virtue
would make the practice of the following ones
all the easier, and chiefly because he would
approach them with habits of virtue already
formed.

He naturally began with the virtue of Temperance, he says, because "it tends to procure that
coolness and clearness of head which is so necessary where constant vigilance was to be kept up,
and a guard maintained against the unremitting
attraction of ancient habits and the force of perpetual temptations."   After Temperance should
be duly attended to, Silence would follow more
easily; and as he wished to gain knowledge
while he likewise improved in virtue, and remembered that it was obtained rather through
the *ear* than by means of the *tongue*, and also

desired to conquer a faulty habit of "prattling, punning, and jesting,"—he gave the second place on his list to Silence.

Then followed Order; by obeying this rule strictly, he was left with time to attend both to his own improvement and to his studies. Next, Resolution; this strengthened the previous habits, and held him firmly on the course of acquiring those which were to follow. Frugality and Industry would help to extricate him from the remainder of his debt, and, by putting him on the road to independence, would make Sincerity, Justice, and the rest of the virtues comparatively easy to acquire.

In order to carry out his plan with regularity,—which alone would make it of much worth to him,—he felt that a daily examination into his heart and conduct would be necessary; and to facilitate this practice to the utmost, he made a little Book, in which he allotted a whole page to each one of the virtues. Each page was ruled with red ink so as to make seven columns,—a column for every day in the week; and he marked each column at the top with a letter for the day. Then he ruled these columns across with thirteen more red lines, placing at the commencement of each line, on the extreme left, the letter signifying one of the virtues, in its due order. And, finally, to carry out his plan, following along on the Virtue line he could make a little black spot under each day of the week, as lettered in the column, for every trespass of which he might find himself guilty against that particular virtue on that particular day.

This plan enabled him to give a week's attention to every one of the virtues in its turn; and he would go through with his catalogue every three months (thirteen weeks), or four times in the course of a year. For example,—his first week's exercise was to keep clear of sinning against the virtue of Temperance; and the next week's, against Silence; the next against Order; and so on to the end. In giving all his attention the first week to Temperance, and trying to avoid all errors against that virtue, he left the other virtues to take their chance, although he was strict to mark down every night the remembered faults of the day. If, too, he could keep his Temperance line clear of spots for the first week, he felt so much strengthened in that virtue as to extend his attention to the next virtue at the same time; and for the next week he would strive to keep *both* lines free from blemishes. Franklin compares his labor over his morals to the work in a garden; the man having a garden to clear does not try to get the weeds all out of the soil at once, but works on one of the beds at a time, and, having got this clean, goes on to the second. And he hoped to persevere with his self-improvement until he could successively clear his lines of all their spots, so that, after going through a number of courses, he should be happy beyond expression in running his eyes over a clean book, after a thirteen weeks' daily search and inquiry.

He prefixed three Mottoes to his little Book,— the first from Addison, the second from Cicero, and the third from the Proverbs of Solomon. That from Addison was taken from his play called 'Cato,' and read thus:

> " Here will I hold. If there's a power above us,
> (And that there is, all nature cries aloud
> Through all her works,)—He must delight in virtue:
> And that which he delights in must be happy."

The motto from Cicero read,—

> "O vitæ Philosophia dux! O virtutum indagatrix expultrixque vitiorum! Unus dies, bene et ex præceptis tuis actus, peccanti immortalitati est anteponendus."

That from the Proverbs read in this way :—

"Length of days is in her right hand, and in her left hand riches and honor. Her ways are ways of pleasantness, and all her paths are peace."

In addition to these significant mottoes, he also prefixed to his examination tables the following little prayer, the product of his own pen :—

"O, powerful Goodness! bountiful Father! merciful Guide! Increase in me that wisdom which discovers my truest interest. Strengthen my resolution to perform what that wisdom dictates. Accept my kind offices to thy other children, as the only return in my power for thy continual favors to me."

There was likewise a little prayer which he extracted from the poet Thomson, and often used in addition to the other.

In order to make the very most of his time and opportunities, he knew that Order required of him to put every part of his business in its proper place and hour; and upon one page of his little book he drew up a scheme, or plan, for occupying the twenty-four hours of any natural day. He divided the day into several parts, thus :—from 5 to 8 in the morning, he set down this rule for himself,—" Rise, wash, and address *Powerful Goodness!* Contrive day's business, and take the resolution of the day; prosecute the present study, and breakfast." From 8 to 12,—" Work." From

12 to 2,—"Read, or look over my accounts, and dine." From 2 to 6,—"Work." From 6 to 10, —"Put things in their places. Supper. Music or diversion, or conversation. Examination of the day." From 10 to 5,—"Sleep." Each morning he asked himself the question, — "What good shall I do to-day?"—and each evening,— "What good have I done to-day?"

For a long time he pursued this rigid course of life and conduct, saving every hour of his time, and undergoing a daily scrutiny at his own hands which few young men, even of those resolutely bent on self-culture, would have had the courage and patience to carry out. It was nothing strange that his little book soon began to remind him how speckled with faults he was. He was obliged to scratch out the marks on his pages in order to use his book over again for a new course; and, in the process, he made holes in the paper. To obviate the necessity of ruling new pages, he used tablets, from whose surface the pencil marks could be readily rubbed out with a wet sponge.

This exercise he kept up for some time, till, at length, instead of going through four courses of self-discipline a year, he went through but one. After that, but one course in several years. And

11

finally, he omitted them altogether, his travelling and voyaging and foreign business preventing such regularity as was necessary to make the thing effective. Still, he always carried his little book about with him, as a reminder of what it was possible for him to attain to. The virtue of Order gave him more trouble than any other; it came the harder for him to practice the habits of this virtue, from the fact that he was not born with a tendency that way. Nor was he more fortunate with the virtue of Method; he had hitherto trusted to his excellent memory, and with the help of that, managed to make things go off well enough; but when he came to setting down to a regular siege before so formidable a virtue, striving to run his parallels closer and closer all the while, he found it cost him so much trouble that he fain would have given it over in despair: he complained of making but slow progress, if any, and of such frequent backslidings, too, that he was like to rest content with a faulty character in at least that regard.

On reviewing his efforts, from time to time, especially when he chanced to fall into a weary mood, he would be strongly tempted to relax them, and to let his more pardonable faults go;

arguing to himself that nobody liked a *perfect* character, even if one were within the reach of man, and that a well-meaning person ought to let just a few faults remain, if only to keep his friends in countenance. So hard a matter is it to live strictly up to the law of perfection, for so much as the term of a single day.

On the subject of Order, he pronounced himself beyond the reach of the arm of discipline. He had little or no hope for himself on that score. When he had grown old, he was made aware of his sad deficiency in this respect, as his memory was not at hand to make up for it; but in regard to the other virtues of his list, he left his emphatic testimony that, though he fell far short of the perfection at which he aimed, he nevertheless was made " a better and a happier man" by attempting it than if he had not tried at all; which reminded him that those who strove to make their handwriting perfect by imitating the engraved copies, though they never made as perfect copies as the originals, still came nearer to the excellence of the standard than if they had never made any attempt to reach it, and greatly improved their hand by the means.

Franklin placed it on record, in his seventy-ninth year, that to this "artifice"—as he termed his self-discipline with the aid of his little book,—he owed, under God's blessing, the constant felicity of his life. To Temperance he declared that he owed his good health and what was left him of a good constitution; to Industry and Frugality, the comfortable circumstances in which he early found himself, as well as the reputation which he enjoyed in the world; and to Sincerity and Justice the confidence which his countrymen reposed in him and the many honorable employments they entrusted to him; while to the whole body, or mass, of these virtues, feeble as was his hold on them at the best, he ascribed that even temper and cheerful habit in conversation which ever attracted to him the company of the young.

In pursuing his course of moral culture, while he strove to be truly religious, he avoided all the creeds of his time; and the reason he gave was simply this,—that "being fully persuaded of the utility and excellency of his (my) method, and that it might be serviceable to people in all religions, and intending some time to publish it, he (I) would not have any thing in it that should prejudice any one, of any sect, against it."

He did purpose to write a little book on these

several virtues, showing the advantages of possessing and the mischiefs of being without them, to be styled " The Art of Virtue ;" and he thought it would have accomplished vastly more good than mere exhortation, since it indicated the *means* and *manner* of obtaining virtue,—but he never found the right opportunity to write and publish his commentary. The many hints he had jotted down to make use of, were laid away till his old age ; his close occupation in early life and his constant public employment later in life preventing his carrying out his plan. But the central idea he proposed to treat of in his little commentary, would have been this, as stated in his own language ;— *"that vicious actions are not hurtful because they are forbidden, but forbidden because they are hurtful."* And he would have proceeded to reason that it was, therefore, every one's interest to be virtuous, who wished to be happy even in this world. He would have further labored to convince young persons " that no qualities are so likely to make a poor man's fortune as those of probity and integrity."

There were but twelve Virtues set down in his catalogue, at first ; but being one day informed by a Quaker friend that people generally thought him

11*

proud, and even insolent and overbearing when conducting an argument, he formed a resolution to try and cure himself of this vice if it could possibly be done; so he added *Humility* to his list, and appended the broadest possible meaning and signification to the word. By recurring to his list of virtues, it will be seen that Humility stands last on the list,—added in consequence of the frank suggestion of his Quaker friend.

To carry out his resolution to keep down every appearance of undue pride, he made a rule never to be too strong in making his own assertions, or to venture upon openly contradicting others. Even in the usual discussions in the Junto, he forbore to use language that implied a fixed opinion, discarding from his phrases such positive words as "certainly" and "undoubtedly," and employing in their place such words as "I conceive", "I apprehend," and "I imagine," or "It so appears to me at present."

When he wished to correct in another what he felt certain to be an error, instead of going at him with a flat contradiction he began by remarking that, under certain circumstances perhaps his opinion would be right, but in the present case *there appeared to him* to be some difference,—and so on. **By** practising this style of speech for a time, he discovered that it **began** to have a marked influence over his manners, and that **he** could indulge quite freely in conversation with **others, on** every variety **of** topic, **with a great** deal of positive pleasure. **This** very modesty made room for his opinions, whereas **a** dogmatic and dictatorial style of speaking **would have** debarred him from **a** hearing at once. **By his** conciliatory manner, too, he **succeeded in winning** over **to his** views many a person who would otherwise have stood out and combated **both himself** and them. **It was but** another **illustration of the old fable of the Sun** and the North Wind, experimenting on **the** traveller in his cloak.

For more than fifty years, beginning with **his** thirtieth year, he records that no one had heard a dogmatical expression escape him. He ascribed **it to this habit, next** perhaps to that **of** integrity, that **he obtained an influence** with **his** fellow-citizens **at so early a day:** he was **a member of the** public councils, and, though **a** bad speaker and halting **in his** language, he rarely **failed to** carry his point.

And this leads him to speak of pride; of which **he says with** marked **emphasis — "Disguise it,**

struggle with it, stifle it, mortify it as much as one pleases, it is still alive, and will every now and then peep out and show itself." He never dared think he had himself overcome it, for then he would only have been *proud* of his *humility*.

CHAPTER VI.

BECOMING A PUBLIC MAN.

HIS continual reading was not without its results, for he read with an object, and not in a desultory manner. He jotted down such thoughts as struck him on the subject of History, and they are preserved. His reflections on one topic, in particular, led him to construct a creed for his own use, which is thus expressed in few words :—

"That there is one God, who made all things.

"That He governs the world by his providence.

"That He ought to be worshipped by adoration, prayer, and thanksgiving.

"But the most acceptable service to God, is doing good to man.

"That the soul is immortal.

"And that God will certainly reward virtue and punish vice, either here or hereafter."

He would have the sect founded on the above

creed spread at first among young men, and single men; each person who was initiated into the same should not only subscribe to the creed, but should also have gone faithfully through the thirteen weeks' examination and practice, according to the schedule described in the previous chapter; the society was to be kept secret for a while, and its several members should look around their young men friends to find those to whom it would be perfectly safe and proper to communicate the scheme. They were to style themselves "The Society of the Free and Easy;" *free* from vice by the practice of the virtues, and, by the practice of industry and frugality *free* from debt, which puts one under constraint, and makes him a sort of slave to his creditors.

Franklin did not make very much headway with his new society, on account of the strict attention he was forced to pay at this time to his business; and the number of his public employments afterward made it impossible for him to take up the scheme—which he always believed an excellent one—and carry it forward to a wide and successful operation.

He published, in the year 1732, a little work which would have given him undying fame among his countrymen, had he written and compiled nothing else; and that was his Almanac, known as "*Poor Richard*." It was at first published under the assumed name of *Richard Saunders;* but as it was repeated year by year, it finally received the name of "Poor Richard's Almanac," and had a life, all together, of about a quarter of a century. His plan was, in making it up, to entertain people while he instructed them; and he brought his shrewd wisdom and irresistible mother-wit to bear upon his project with wonderful success. "Poor Richard" came to be in such demand that he sold every year as many as ten thousand copies, and reaped a generous profit from his labor. It was one of those productions which fitted exactly into the wants of the times, and therefore became at once popular.

Seeing how eagerly it was read, and that there was no locality within reach to which it did not penetrate, as a welcome friend, he conceived the idea of engrafting upon it, as a mere Almanac, a body of homely and quaint sentiments and mottoes, filled with the meat of meaning, which could not so easily be found by the common people anywhere else. It became, therefore, a sort of library of wisdom,—a compendium of common sense,—

a storehouse of wise and homely proverbs, — to
which everybody could go, and freely help himself to such as he wanted. As he described the
contents himself, he says—"I filled all the little
spaces that occurred between the remarkable days
in the calendar with proverbial sentences, chiefly
by such as inculcated industry and frugality as the
means of procuring wealth and thereby securing
virtue; it being more difficult for a man in want
to act always honestly, as, to use here one of those
proverbs, *it is hard for an empty sack to stand upright.*"

It is not to be thought, however, that the proverbs uttered each year by "Poor Richard" were
the coin of Franklin's brain; they contained, on
the contrary, the wisdom of many ages and many
nations. Franklin assembled them into a connected discourse, which he prefixed to the Almanac of 1757, as a wise and shrewd old man's harangue to the people gathered at an auction; and
by thus bringing these bits of sage counsel together, he believed he could make a greater
impression.

Nor was he at fault in his calculation. He
enjoyed the satisfaction of seeing the piece copied
in all the newspapers of the country, and printed

again on large sheets of paper in England, where they were stuck up on the walls of the dwellings. It was translated into French, and large numbers of the printed sheets were purchased by the clergy and gentry to distribute among their poor parishioners and tenants. The effect of it was such in the province of Pennsylvania that it was believed it put a stop, in a degree, to the use of foreign luxuries, in consequence of which there was a great deal more money kept at home than was ever known before.

A few of the more current proverbs and "wise saws" are given here, from this famous production. It is to be remembered, however, that they are taken from the lips (in imagination) of a white-haired old man who is attending an auction sale of a broken merchant's goods, and to whom the bystanders put the questions — "Pray, Father Abraham, what think ye of the times? Won't these heavy taxes quite ruin the country? How shall we ever be able to pay them? What would you advise us to?" The old man stood up and answered them—"If you'd have my advice, I'll give it to you in short; 'for a word to the wise is enough, and many words won't fill a bushel,' as Poor Richard says."

12

The old man goes on to speak of the taxes; and tells his listeners that if those laid by the government were *the only ones* we had to pay, they would get along very well; they were taxed twice as much by their *idleness*, three times as much by their *pride*, and four times as much by their *folly*. And, upon this, he quotes Poor Richard as saying—"God helps those who help themselves." "Sloth, like rust, consumes faster than labor wears; while the key often used is always bright." "Dost thou love life? then do not squander time, for that's the stuff life is made of." "The sleeping fox catches no poultry, and there will be sleeping enough in the grave." "Lost time is never found again; and what we call time enough, always proves little enough." "Sloth makes all things difficult, but industry all easy." "He that rises late must trot all day, and shall scarce overtake his business at night; while Laziness travels so slow that Poverty soon overtakes him." "Drive thy business; let not that drive thee."

And the old man tells them further, that nothing is mended by the wishing; it must needs come by work. There is no use in wishing the times were better; we *make* them better, if we bestir ourselves. "Industry needs not wish,"—as Poor

Richard says. "He that lives upon hope will die fasting." "There are no gains without pains." "He that hath a trade, hath an estate : and he that hath a calling, hath an office of profit and honor." "At the workingman's house hunger looks in, but dare not enter." "Industry pays debts, but despair increaseth them." "Diligence is the mother of good luck;" and "God gives all things to industry; then plow deep while sluggards sleep, and you will have corn to sell and keep." "One to-day is worth two to-morrows." "Handle your tools without mittens." "The cat in gloves catches no mice." "Continual dropping wears away stones, and by diligence and patience the mouse ate into the cable, and light strokes fell great oaks."

When the old man is asked if we are to afford ourselves no leisure, he answers in proverbs again —"Employ thy time well if thou meanest to gain leisure; and since thou art not sure of a minute, throw not away an hour." "A life of leisure and a life of laziness are two things." "Troubles spring from idleness, and grievous toils from needless ease; many without labor would live by their own wits only; but they break for want of stock." "Fly pleasures, and they will follow you; the diligent spinner has a large shift." But one must needs be settled and steady, or all his industry goes for little or nothing; there, as Poor Richard says,—"Three removes are as bad as a fire." "Keep thy shop, and thy shop will keep thee." "If you would have your business done, go; if not, send." "The eye of the master will do more work than both his hands." "Want of care does us more damage than want of knowledge." "Not to oversee workmen is to leave them your purse open." "If you would have a faithful servant, and one that you like, serve yourself." "A little neglect may breed a great mischief." "For want of a nail, the shoe was lost; for want of a shoe, the horse was lost; and for want of a horse, the rider was lost; being overtaken and slain by the enemy—all for want of care about a horse-shoe nail."

Then he talks to his listeners upon Frugality, showing them that they must practice frugality if they would make their industry successful. And he proceeds to quote Poor Richard as saying—"A fat kitchen makes a lean will." "If you would be wealthy, think of saving as well as getting." "What maintains one vice would bring up two children." "Beware of little expense; a small leak will sink a great ship." "Who dainties love shall beggars prove." "Fools make feasts, and wise men eat them."

Speaking to the people about coming to an auction sale to purchase goods because they expected to find them cheap, the old man warns them that, if they do not look out, they will find their *goods* to be *evils;* and he reminds them again of what Poor Richard says,—"Buy what thou hast no need of, and ere long thou shalt sell thy necessaries." And again,—"It is foolish to lay out money in a purchase of repentance." "Silks and satins, scarlets and velvets put out the kitchen fire." "For one poor person, there are a hundred indigent." "A ploughman on his legs is higher than a gentleman on his knees." On the subject of small spendings for needless things, the old man quotes Poor Richard as saying—"A child and a fool imagine twenty shillings and twenty years can never be spent; but always be taking out of the meal-tub, and never putting in, soon comes to the bottom." "When the well is dry, they know the worth of water." "If you would know the value of money, go and try to borrow some; for he that goes a-borrowing goes a-sorrowing." "Pride is as loud a beggar as Want, and a great deal more

12*

saucy." "It is easier to suppress the first desire than to satisfy all that follow it." "Pride that dines on vanity, sups on contempt." And again, —"Pride breakfasted with Plenty, dined with Poverty, and supped with Infamy."

On the subject of running in debt, the old man scatters the pearls of his proverbs among the crowd in this wise:—"The second vice is lying; the first is running in debt." "Lying rides on debt's back." "It is hard for an empty sack to stand upright." "Creditors have better memories than debtors;" and, once more, "Creditors are a superstitious sect, great observers of set days and times." "Those have a short Lent, who owe money to be paid at Easter." "For age and want save while you may,—No morning sun lasts a whole day." And telling the crowd about him that gain may be temporary and uncertain, but expense is ever constant and certain, he quotes Poor Richard as saying—"It is easier to build two chimneys than to keep one in fuel." "Rather go to bed supperless than rise in debt."

And after exhorting them not to trust, either to industry, frugality, and prudence altogether, which can help no one without the attendant blessing of Heaven,—he concludes his pithy and impressive address with a handful of summary injunctions, which may be called the marrow of the matter, thus:—"And now, to conclude, 'Experience keeps a dear school; but fools will learn in no other, and scarce in that; for it is true, we may give advice, but we cannot give conduct,' as Poor Richard says. However, remember this, 'They that will not be counselled cannot be helped,' as Poor Richard says; and, farther, that 'If you will not hear Reason, she will surely rap your knuckles.'"

And thus the old gentleman ended his harangue. But he says that the people assembled at the auction went on and bought just as if he had not spoken to them at all, paying no heed to his proverbs and precepts.

We have given this sample of "Poor Richard," because it was such a famous affair in its day, and its name lives after it. Probably no book, large or small, printed in America through the whole of the last century, had such influence over the popular mind. Its shrewd wisdom commended it to all thoughtfully-inclined persons, while its dry humor and story-telling counsels attracted and impressed those who would have been reached by no other style of address.

Franklin employed his newspaper, too, in imparting the same sort of moral instruction. Sometimes he printed choice extracts from Addison's Spectator, and at other times he enlivened its columns with short pieces which he had first composed and read to the Junto; among the rest, imaginary dialogues, discourses, and essays. At this time, he was not yet thirty years of age.

He never used his columns for spreading scandal; it was his opinion that personal altercations and abuse were become too common, and reflected only disgrace on the community; and he made a worthy effort to put an end to the practice and to hold up a better example. Oftentimes he was urged by one and another to print in the paper some attack which they wished to make on other persons; and when he denied them their request, they would bring up the illustration of the stage-coach, saying that a newspaper was just like that, in which any one who paid had a right to a place; but he stopped further importunities by telling them that if they wished, he would print their pieces separately, and they might take as many copies as they wanted.

He sent off one of his journeymen to Charleston, in 1733, where he heard a printer was wanted, supplying him with a press. The agreement was, that Franklin was to pay one-third the expense of the business, and have one-third of the profits. The man did not make returns of his business with any regularity, and after a time died, leaving matters entirely unsettled and loose between them; but his wife, who was born and bred in Holland, and who had learned how to keep accounts, took charge of the affairs of her late husband, and sent him a plain statement of past transactions as well as regular business reports every three months afterward. So successfully did she manage the business, she brought up a family of children with credit, and finally bought out Franklin's share in the concern and set up her son at the head of it.

About this time, he had an adventure with a Presbyterian minister who had lately come to Philadelphia to preach. He was a young man, with a fine voice, who drew to himself a crowd of admiring hearers from the different denominations by his extemporaneous addresses. His discourses pleased Franklin too, from the fact that they were not of a dogmatical cast, but held up continually the need of "good works." Some of the more "orthodox" Presbyterians, with the

older ministers, not liking his doctrine, brought
him before the Synod on a charge of preaching
heretical doctrines, and desired to have him
silenced. Franklin took up for him with much
zeal, writing and talking for him, and laboring to
build up a party which would sustain him. But
finding, as he relates, that, "though an elegant
preacher, he was but a poor writer," he wrote for
him two or three pamphlets together with a piece
in the newspaper. But while the contest raged,
it turned out that one of his adversaries remembered to have somewhere read a part of one of
the most admired sermons which he had preached;
and, on looking the matter up, it turned out that
he had been preaching a discourse, or the greater
part of one, from a British clergyman, which had
been before published in one of the Reviews.
The friends of the young minister were sickened
with this discovery, and at once abandoned him
and his cause in disgust. But this was not the
case with Franklin; with his usual shrewdness,
he stuck by him, giving as a reason that he was
much more in favor of his giving them good discourses, though composed by another, than poor
ones composed by himself! But the case went
against him, nevertheless. Before he left the

town, the young minister frankly confessed to Franklin that he had not only stolen that sermon, but all his sermons, in the same way: his memory being such that he was able to retain and repeat any sermon after a single reading only. Franklin left the congregation soon after the minister went, and never worshipped with it again, though he paid over his subscription for the support of its ministers for many years.

To qualify himself for such positions in life as he might be placed in, in the future, he began to study the languages about this time, and led off with the French; and he very soon became so much a master of that tongue as to be able to read the books in it with ease and readiness. He next went upon Italian. A friend happened to be studying it at the same time, who used to often beg Franklin to play chess with him: but finding the game was taking up too much of his time, he told his friend he would play no more except on this condition,—that the one who won the game should have the right to impose on the other a stated task, either in the grammar, which was to be learned by heart, or in translating,—the same to be performed by the time of the next meeting. They were so evenly matched at the game that, as Franklin said, they fairly "*beat* one another into that language." With a little pains and industry, he in time acquired sufficient knowledge of Spanish to read books written in that tongue likewise.

After having thus gone into modern languages, he was greatly surprised, on looking into a Latin Testament, to find that he already understood more of that language than he had imagined. He had had a year's instruction in a Latin School, in his youth, but never pursued his early acquaintance with the tongue; he was now encouraged, however, to go at the study once more, and found his way made smooth by his previous success with the more modern languages. From which fact he came to the conclusion that we generally pursue just the wrong course in the study of the languages, by beginning with the Latin. His judgment was, that it was better to begin with the French, and proceed to the Italian and the Latin. For if the young student should never proceed farther than French, that language he would afterwards find of use to him; but if, beginning with Latin, he stopped with that, his attainment would be of no practical value.

By this time he had been absent from Boston,

his native place, ten long years; changes had taken place in that period, and, among the rest, he found himself in easy circumstances. He determined to go and make a visit to his relatives at the East. He said he never could afford the expense of such a journey before now. He says nothing of his visit to Boston, however, but mentions an incident which occurred at Newport, Rhode Island, where he stopped on his return to see his brother James, from whom he had run away years before. Their meeting was cordial and affectionate, all their former differences having been forgotten. The brother was still engaged in the printing business there, but his health was giving way, and he was looking for the approach of his end. Weighed down with this apprehension, he requested his brother Benjamin to take home his son with him, then a lad of but ten years, and bring him up to the printing business. This he promised to do, and did do: although he sent the boy to school for a few years before putting him to work in the office. While the lad was thus engaged learning his trade, his mother was carrying on the business at Newport to the best of her skill; and when he had finally qualified himself to be a printer, his Uncle Benja-

13

min furnished him with an assortment of new types, and enabled him to take the business at Newport off his mother's hands and carry it on himself. Franklin felt that in this way he made amends for the loss and trouble to which he subjected his older brother, when he ran away from him to Philadelphia.

In the year 1736, he lost a little son, but four years old, by the small-pox. He had never been inoculated, which made it very difficult for the father to forgive himself for his neglect.

The same year, he was chosen Clerk of the General Assembly. There was no opposition to him that year; though when his name was proposed for the same office, the next year, a new member of the Assembly got up and made a long and loud speech against him, having a candidate of his own to bring forward. Franklin was chosen, however. His pay as Clerk was of some assistance to him at that time; but the interest for his business which an acquaintance with the members enabled him to make, was better than all. They voted that he should do about the whole of the House printing —the votes, the laws, the paper money, and the other public jobs, great and small, which proved very profitable. The member who had risen and opposed him for the clerkship Franklin was desirous of appeasing, for he was a gentleman of fortune, well educated, and possessed of talents that were likely to give him influence over the House in the future. Instead, however, of fawning upon him, he tried a trick of innocent flattery; hearing that he had a certain rare and curious book in his library, he wrote him a note, saying that he heard the gentleman had such a book, and requesting the favor of its loan for a few days. The book was lent him, of course; Franklin returned it in about a week, with many thanks, which he expressed with care in another note. The gentleman came over and spoke to him the next time the house met,—a thing he had never done before,—accosting him with great civility. The result of it was, he ever afterwards showed a willingness to serve Franklin in such way as he could, and they struck up a friendship that lasted until death.

The postmaster-general of the provinces, Governor Spotswood, late Governor of Virginia, was not altogether satisfied with his Philadelphia deputy, and in 1737 he removed him and appointed Franklin to his place. The former incumbent had been guilty of negligence in sending in his office accounts, and of want of exactness in drawing them up. Franklin accepted the office without hesitation, and found it of great help to him every way. The salary it returned him was by no means large, but it afforded him a good many favorable opportunities to supply his newspaper with correspondence and advertisements both, while it also enabled him to increase his circulation. The opposition paper began to decline as the Gazette advanced; but Franklin remembered his resolve, taken when he was in "the day of small things" himself, not to treat a rival as scurvily as the former post-master had treated him. He therefore permitted the post-riders to carry the other papers just as freely as they did his own.

His mind now turned more actively to public matters than ever. He began with paying attention to small affairs; but by doing his duty to those well and thoroughly, he qualified himself for that wider field to which he was destined not long afterward to be called. First, he looked into the city watch business. The constables of the different wards took turns in managing it. Each summoned a certain number of housekeepers to go around the town with him during the night. We have to smile, recalling these primitive customs and contrasting them with the day and night police system of the present time.

Franklin found, on investigation, that such as chose to pay the constable six shillings a year to be excused, which sum was popularly thought to go for hiring substitutes, could be let off entirely. But that sum he found to be a great deal more than sufficient to hire all the substitutes that were wanted, the amount left over furnishing the constable taking it a handsome little profit; the only money which the latter spent being for a little drink, with which he used to hire such men to patrol the streets along with him as the respectable portion of the citizens did not choose to mix with. Besides, they did not walk their rounds, either; they would collect at some place, and pass the night in tippling.

The matter was first brought up by Franklin in the Junto. He wrote a paper on it, setting forth the wretched way in which watch was kept for the town, but showing up more especially the injustice of exacting the sum of six shillings per head from every person who expected to derive benefit from the assessment; for a poor widow, whose whole property might not amount to more than fifty pounds, was taxed just as much toward sup-

13*

porting the watch as the merchant who had thousands of pounds' worth of goods in his stores. He proposed, instead of this, the hiring of proper men to serve at the business constantly; and his plan was, to pay them their wages by taxing *property*, rather than *persons*. The idea took well with the Junto, and was communicated to all the other clubs which had sprung from it and were still connected with it. And although, as a distinct plan, it was not immediately carried into execution, it nevertheless set matters in such a train that after a time the people of Philadelphia settled upon it as a fixed policy; and great good came from it to all interests.

Franklin likewise paid attention, at this time, to the causes of fires, and the best modes of preventing as well as extinguishing them. He wrote a paper on the subject, and published it in the Gazette. It took well with the people at large, and led to the formation of a company of citizens for the rapid extinguishment of fires,—or what we should now style a "fire company." Thirty in all joined it at first, whose business was to be not only the speedy putting out of fires but the saving of goods also, when in danger. Each member was required to keep at hand a certain number of leather buckets, in good order and fit for use, together with strong bags and baskets for removing goods; and all were to be brought to every fire that broke out. About once a month they passed a social evening together, engaged chiefly in talking on fires and the readiest way to overcome their destructiveness.

So well were the citizens pleased with the new idea, they banded together to form other companies; and at length the greater part of the men of property in town were included in one or another of these most useful organizations. At least fifty years after Franklin formed the first association, then known as the "Union Fire Association," it was still in existence; and at that time all but one, besides Franklin, were dead. The fines which were levied found them in ladders, fire hooks, and engines; and for the long period of half a century, so excellent was the system, the city never lost by fire more than two houses at a time.

CHAPTER VII.

GEORGE WHITFIELD — SOLDIERING — A PHILOSOPHER.

THE famous preacher, George Whitfield, came to Philadelphia in 1739, from Ireland. His fame as a revival preacher had gone before him. In the course of his life, he crossed the Atlantic a great many times, for a man of that generation, and seemed drawn to the people of America by very strong ties. When he first made his appearance in Philadelphia, the clergy permitted him to hold forth in their churches; but after a time they fell out with him for some reason, and he was obliged to assemble his auditory in the open fields.

People of every denomination and belief flocked to hear him. He called assemblies about him, to listen to his masterly harangues, such as the men of that day had never beheld. They gathered at the sound of his voice in battalions, by the thousands and tens of thousands. Franklin used to wonder how they had patience to listen to him, when he was continually flinging the most savage denunciations in their faces, and telling them that by nature they were "half beasts and half devils." But there was an almost weird magnetism about this remarkable man, holding others spell-bound by the very tones of his voice. His declamatory power was indescribable. The effect immediately produced upon the popular mind it is not easy to reproduce in narrative. Everybody seemed to have suddenly become deeply concerned for his soul. The town dropped its habit of indifference and levity, and put on an air of the most serious thoughtfulness. Franklin describes it—"it seemed as if *all the world* were growing religious, so that one could not walk through the town in an evening without hearing psalms sung in different families of every street."

After a time, it was found inconvenient to continue these monster meetings in the open air, on account of the inclement weather as well as for other reasons; and it was proposed to build a house of some sort, that should accommodate all who wished to hear the new apostle. Money was very speedily contributed, in sums sufficient to purchase ground and erect a building one hundrcd feet long and seventy broad; and the citizens fell to the work with such zeal that it was completed long before they had any of them believed it possible. The whole property was placed in the hands of trustees, the condition being that it should be used for the accommodation " of any preacher of any religious persuasion," who might ever wish to speak to the people of Philadelphia. The design was, to accommodate the people rather than the sects; so that, as Franklin expressed it, "even if the Mufti of Constantinople were to send a missionary to preach Mahometanism to us, he would find a pulpit at his service."

Whitfield went south, as far as Georgia, after leaving Philadelphia, preaching as he went. He collected crowds around him wherever he stopped to exhort, and left impressions that outlasted even the generation which listened to his tumultuous words. After going among the people of the then new colony of Georgia and becoming thoroughly acquainted with their situation, he was deeply impressed with the fact that they were in an almost helpless condition, and resolved to come back and solicit charity on their behalf. The preacher's plan was to build an orphan asylum for the numbers of poor children that were left destitute by the misfortunes of their parents; and large and generous collections were immediately sent in on behalf of this project.

It appears that the early colonists of Georgia were made up of broken-down London shop-keepers and insolvent debtors: men who could do nothing more for themselves or their families at home, and of whom still less might be expected abroad, especially in a wilderness. Many of these settlers had been taken from the common jails in the old country, and were of fixed and unchange-able habits of idleness. Such a class of persons, on being set down in the woods with their families, could hardly be expected to hew their way through the surrounding roughness to com-fort and plenty. In consequence of this inability to help themselves, therefore, they perished by scores, leaving a crowd of miserable children behind to be assisted by charity or to die.

Whitfield's plan, on his return to Pennsylvania, was to provide a grand asylum for these children of want, and he had, as already mentioned, col-lected large sums for that purpose in Philadel-phia. Franklin lent his sympathy to the project, but he thought it better that the building in question should be erected in Philadelphia than off in Georgia, and that the children should be brought North. There was another consideration: if it were to be built in Georgia, a large number of mechanics would have to go out there from Philadelphia, and Franklin was averse to letting so valuable an element of their own colony go away. He therefore refused to contribute a cent to the project, Whitfield meantime just as stoutly refusing to listen to his suggestion to build the asylum at Philadelphia.

While thus resolute against giving the great preacher anything to help him on, Franklin pleasantly narrates a characteristic incident that concerns each of the parties to it about equally:—
"I happened soon after to attend one of his (Whitfield's) sermons, in the course of which I perceived he intended to finish with a collection; and I silently resolved he should get nothing from me. I had, in my pocket, a handful of copper money, three or four silver dollars, and five pistoles in gold. As he proceeded, *I began to soften*, and concluded to give the copper. Another stroke of his oratory made me ashamed of that, and determined me to give the silver; and he finished so admirably, that *I emptied my pocket wholly into the collector's dish, gold and all.* At this

sermon there was also one of our club, who, being of my sentiments respecting the building in Georgia, and suspecting a collection might be intended, had, by precaution, emptied his pockets before he came from home. Towards the conclusion of the discourse, however, he felt a strong inclination to give, and applied to a neighbor, who stood near him, to lend him some money for the purpose. The request was fortunately made to perhaps the only man in the company who had the firmness not to be affected by the preacher. His answer was, '*At any other time*, friend Hopkinson, I would lend to thee freely; but not now; for thee seems to be out of thy right senses.'"

Franklin says there was a suspicion with some that Mr. Whitfield would apply the contributions he obtained to his own uses; but, for himself, he never harbored such a thought. He was more or less intimate with the great preacher, and printed his sermons and journals for him; and he believed him to be a thoroughly honest man, incapable of taking any such mean advantage of his position. Their friendship was sincere, and lasted as long as both lived. Whitfield used to put up prayers for Franklin's conversion, but the latter says " he never had the satisfaction of believing that his

14

prayers were heard." To illustrate the character of their friendship, Franklin relates the following anecdote:—" Upon one of his arrivals from England at Boston, he wrote to me that he should come soon to Philadelphia, but knew not where he could lodge when there, as he understood his old friend and host, Mr. Benezet, was removed to Germantown. My answer was, 'You know my house; if you can make shift with its scanty accommodations, you will be most heartily welcome.' He replied, that if I made that kind offer for *Christ's* sake, I should not miss of a reward. And I returned, 'Don't let me be mistaken; it was not for *Christ's* sake, but for *your sake*.'"

According to Franklin's account, the great preacher had a loud and clear voice, and articulated every word so perfectly that he could be heard and understood a great ways. One evening, while he was preaching from the Court House steps in the middle of Market street, Franklin had the curiosity to test the power of his voice, which he did in the following ingenious manner. Both Market and Second streets were filled to a considerable distance. Franklin was on the further edge of the crowd in Market street, and kept retreating gradually toward the river. He could hear Whitfield's voice with distinctness until he came near Front street, where the noise of that street obscured it. With this basis of calculation, he imagined a semicircular space, of which a direct line from himself to the preacher should be the radius, filled with people; and, by allowing two square feet to each person, he calculated that he could be heard by more than thirty thousand people. This estimate inclined him to believe the stories which had been told of Whitfield's having preached to twenty-five thousand people in the fields.

Franklin found he could soon detect one of his new discourses from an old one; the latter was much better delivered, owing to the practice obtained in repeating it so many times. He says that "every accent, every emphasis, every modulation of voice was so perfectly well turned and well placed, that, without being interested in the subject, one could not help being pleased with the discourse, — a pleasure of much the same kind with that received from an excellent piece of music."

The printing business of Franklin was rapidly increasing, and he was becoming a man of means and a substantial citizen. He now saw the actual fruits of frugality, industry, and perseverance.

His plans had thus far resulted just as he would have had them. He writes of himself that he now experienced the truth of an old remark, "that, after getting the first hundred pounds, it is more easy to get the second,"—money having a wonderful faculty of multiplying itself. He engaged at this time in several partnerships, having found the one in South Carolina so profitable. Such of his workmen as had behaved well he sent off into other colonies, and helped them to establish printing-houses; the larger part of them turned out prosperously, being able, at the end of the term of their engagement (six years), to purchase the types of Franklin for themselves. In no single partnership of this sort did he find himself with a quarrel on his hands; they were all carried on, and all ended, amicably. The great reason for this good fortune he ascribed to the fact that, in making engagements of this sort, every part of the contract was clearly laid down and so well understood in the first place, that there was no possibilities of any future falling out. And this point Franklin especially enjoins upon all persons who are thinking of forming partnerships; "for," says he, "whatever esteem partners may have for, or confidence in, each other at the time of the contract, little jealousies and disgusts may arise, with ideas of inequality in the care and burden, business, etc., which are attended often with breach of friendship and of the connection ; perhaps with lawsuits and other disagreeable consequences."

There were two prime wants in the Pennsylvania colony, at this time, which Franklin turned his attention to, in the hope of having them speedily supplied ; there was no militia system, and no college. The one was of the first importance as a matter of defence for the colony in these troubled times, and the other was needed for the proper education of youth. In the year 1743, he drew up a plan for founding an academy, and made an effort to obtain a teacher ; but the scheme was laid aside for that year, and, in the following year, he brought forward with success his plans for establishing a "Philosophical Society."

Spain was at war with Great Britain at this time, and France had just joined her; this state of affairs led the first citizens of Pennsylvania colony to look around and see how they could ward off danger from their boundaries. The Governor of the colony, Thomas, had urged the Assembly (which was composed of Quakers) in vain to pass a militia law and make provision for defence ; and

Franklin resolved to try voluntary contributions. For this purpose he printed a pamplet, to which he gave the name PLAIN TRUTH; and in the course of it he set forth their helpless condition and urged the need of immediate steps for defence, adding that in a few days he should propose an association to the people at large.

The pamphlet produced just the right effect. The citizens without hesitation called upon the author for his plan of association. He drew it up hastily in connection with a few friends, and called a general town meeting in the big building which had been erected for liberal preaching. He had previously prepared a number of copies of his new plan, and placed pens and ink about the room where access could readily be had to them. Then after addressing the people on the subject, he caused copies of his draft to be circulated, and called on the people to subscribe their names without reserve. On counting up these names, after the meeting adjourned, it was found that *twelve hundred* men had subscribed to the new agreement; and after sending it abroad over the country, the plan received the signatures of more than ten thousand colonists!

This was a good beginning. The "Plain Truth"

pamphlet had thus far done a noble work. This large body of men provided themselves as soon as they could with arms, formed themselves into companies, chose officers, and met every week for drill. The women, not to be outdone in patriotism, made silk colors for the several companies, painting and working upon them such devices and mottoes as Franklin supplied them with.

The officers of the regiment which was formed in Philadelphia, met and chose Franklin their Colonel. He felt that he was not qualified for the post, and desired them to appoint a Mr. Lawrence —a gentleman of influence—in his place, which they finally did. The first thing to be done, after this, was the erection of a battery below the town and mounting it with cannon. The problem was, how to supply the cannon. Franklin, whose wits seemed always about him, proposed *a lottery* for the purpose of defraying the expense of building the battery; and the tickets were soon taken up, and the work on the battery speedily begun. The defenses were merely of logs, filled in with earth.

The citizens bought some cannon in Boston; and sent to London for some; when they sent over to the latter place, they put in their claims before the Proprietaries of the province, hoping to in-

duce them to offer their assistance to the young
settlement also. Col. Lawrence, Franklin, and
two other gentlemen meanwhile went to New
York, commissioned to ask of Gov. Clinton, in
the name of the association, a few pieces of cannon,—as many as they could get from him. At
first, the Governor plumply refused; but he was
again plied with their requests, while at dinner
with his Council, where much good old Madeira
was drunk, and he relented so far as to consent
to loan *six*. The wine still going round, he agreed
to let *ten* go; and, at last, becoming still more
mellow, he consented to part with *eighteen*. They
were good pieces, eighteen-pounders, and mounted
on carriages. They were taken forthwith across
to Philadelphia, mounted on the battery, and all
ready for the approach of an enemy. A watch
was kept up by the signers to the military association, every night during the continuance of the
war; and Franklin took his turn with the rest, in
pacing his weary walk beneath the stars. It was
his first experience as a common soldier.

Seeing of what worth he was in the community,
the Governor and Council immediately took him
into their confidence, and freely consulted him in
every instance where they believed they could fur-

ther the plans of the military organization. With his many other suggestions, he proposed that a Fast Day should be observed, as was the custom at stated times in New England. He would have them ask the blessing of Heaven on their undertaking. The Governor not being familiar with the forms, and the Secretary being just as ignorant of them, recourse was had to Franklin, who drew the proclamation after the New England style; it was next translated into German and scattered through the province.

Some of his friends feared that Franklin's activity in these war matters would make him unpopular with the Quakers, who were practically peace men, and who had a large majority in the Assembly. One young man, who had friends in that body, and wished to be elected to the Clerkship himself, came and told him that it was determined to defeat him at the next session; and rather than see him disgraced in that way, he coolly advised him to resign. Franklin informed him, in reply, that he had once heard, or read, of a public man who made it a rule never to ask for an office, and never to refuse it when offered him. "I approve," said he, "of this rule, and shall practice it with a small addition; I shall never *ask*, never *refuse*, and never *resign* an office." This was plump and plain; and his mousing competitor must have gone away satisfied. Franklin, however, was chosen Clerk at the next session; they could find no other reason for defeating him than his connection with the war association, and they did not care to put their action on that ground. His testimony goes to show, in fact, that Quakers would fight on the *defensive*, at any rate.

He relates one anecdote which illustrates their peculiar feeling at that time. At a meeting of their Fire Company,—the same which he had originated or set on foot,—it was proposed to take the sixty pounds which belonged to the company and invest it in lottery tickets for the erection of the battery below the town. The matter had to be laid over for discussion till the next meeting. In the fire company were thirty members, twenty-two of whom were Quakers. The eight outside ones were very punctual at the meeting, although they had no idea of carrying Quakers enough with them to make up a majority for the project. Only one Quaker, however, appeared to oppose the scheme; he was sorry the thing had been brought up, for the Friends were all against it, and the fire company was in danger of being broken up by it

He was answered, however, that nothing was easier than for the Quakers to vote down the rest, as they clearly outnumbered them, and the will of the majority would of course be submitted to. At last the hour came for bringing the matter to a vote. Mr. Morris admitted that the rules allowed them to do it, but there were a number not then present, who intended to come in and vote against it, and it would be only fair to give them time to assemble. Just at this moment, a servant came in and communicated to Franklin that a couple of gentlemen below would like to speak with him. He went down and found two members of the company, Quakers. They told him there were eight of them in a tavern close at hand, and that they were all of them ready to come in and vote for the proposal if it should be necessary, although they would prefer not to be called upon if it could be managed without them, since it would make trouble for them with their friends.

Franklin went back up stairs feeling easier; for now he knew that he could carry a majority with him in any case. He could afford to be magnanimous, therefore, and agreed to wait another hour, knowing well enough that a majority of his opponents would never come in. Mr. Morris ad mitted that this second delay was extremely fair. But after much waiting it was found that not one of his side came in, and of course there was no need of sending for the men at the tavern. So at the expiration of the hour the motion was put and carried, by a vote of *eight* to *one!* This showed how peaceful even Quakers were, when a war pinch came.

The Quaker, too, who placed the sixty pounds in Franklin's hands to purchase the lottery tickets with,—Mr. Logan,—wrote a pamphlet in favor of *defensive* war. In the course of his many conversations with Franklin, he told him the following anecdote of his old master, William Penn, bearing directly on that point: He came over from England with him when a young man, as his Secretary. As it was in a time of war, the ship they came in was chased by an armed vessel which was supposed to be an enemy. The captain made ready for defending his craft, but told Penn and his company of Quakers that, as he did not expect any help from them during the conflict, they were at liberty to retire into the cabin. All of them complied with the suggestion, except young Logan; he preferred to stay on deck and assist at the defence; and the officer appointed him to a place at one of the guns. But it turned out that the enemy was *no* enemy, and there was therefore no fighting to do. When, however, the young Secretary went below to communicate the news to William Penn, the latter administered to him a stern rebuke for doing as he had done,—remaining upon deck and offering to take a part in the defence; and reminded him that it was contrary to the principles of the Friends. Logan did not exactly like to be rebuked in this style by his master, before all the company. So he answered to him—"I being thy servant, why did thee not order me to come down? But thee was willing enough that I should stay and help to fight the ship, *when thee thought there was danger!*"

Franklin was many times amused, while in the Assembly, to observe the little subterfuges and excuses they resorted to, in order to help on the Crown in matters of war, when called on for aid; they were patriotic at heart, but peaceful on principle; they hated to refuse the government, and still would not offend one another by transgressing their own religious rules: whenever the Assembly, therefore,—which was by a large majority Quaker,—voted money for the defence of the province, it always took pains to word the grant as

15

"for the King's use," but making no mention
how it was to be applied. When powder was
wanted for the garrison at Louisburg, and New
England begged it of Pennsylvania, they refused
to grant money to buy powder, because that was
an article of war; but they roguishly voted to
place three thousand pounds in the hands of the
Governor, and appropriate it for the purchase of
bread, flour, wheat, or *other grain*. Some of the
Council, with the hope of embarrassing the Governor, advised him not to accept *provision*, as that
was not what he had asked from the Assembly;
but he said he should do it nevertheless, "for I
understand very well their meaning; *other grain*
is gunpowder." And the "other grain" was
bought by him for New England, and no objection
made to it, either.

Had the proposal before the fire company—to
invest the company's money in lottery tickets—
failed to pass, Franklin said he should have
moved to purchase a *fire engine* with it; and, if
that plan had passed, he should have bought a
"*great gun*," which is a *fire engine*, beyond a
doubt.

Having invented, only three or four years
before, an open stove for the better warming of

rooms and the saving of fuel, he presented his model to his friend, Robert Grace, who owned a furnace and found the casting of the stove plates very profitable, the stoves being in active demand. In order to extend the sale of his new stove still more, he wrote and published a pamphlet, styled —"An Account of the new-invented Pennsylvanian Fire-places," &c., &c. The pamphlet had an excellent effect in the direction intended. The Governor was so well pleased with the construction of the stove, from merely reading its description in the pamphlet, that he offered to give Franklin a patent, with the sole right to sell all the stoves manufactured under it, for three years to come; but the latter declined the gift, in obedience to a rule which he says ever weighed with him on such occasions,—"that, as we enjoy great advantages from the inventions of others, we should be glad of an opportunity to serve others by any invention of ours; and this we should do freely and generously."

The "Franklin Stove" was known to the people of the present generation, and remained an ornament in many a parlor and living-room until coal so generally superseded the use of wood.

We may now consider Franklin well started on his career as a Philosopher. In the succeeding chapter, we shall show how he applied his inventive talent and acute observation to the devising of various schemes by which his fellow-citizens would be made more comfortable and happy.

CHAPTER VIII.

GETTING FAME.

AS soon as the war was over, Franklin gave over all further thought about the Association, of course; and the next plan to which he turned his attention was the establishment of an Academy. To bring the matter before the public, he first associated himself with a number of friends from the Junto, and next published a pamphlet, styled "Proposals relating to the Education of Youth in Pennsylvania." By distributing this freely among the people, without cost, he prepared their minds for the proposal which he was all ready to make to them; which was, to start a subscription for opening and supporting an academy, the sums subscribed by each person to be paid in yearly instalments for five years. He believed that he could raise more money by dividing the burden in this way. Nor,

15*

indeed, was his calculation out of the way, for he secured about five thousand pounds.

He did not bring *himself* forward as the author of the scheme, and therefore secured for it more immediate favor. The subscribers chose twenty-four trustees to carry the plan out, and appointed the Attorney-General, Mr. Francis, and himself, to draft a proper Constitution. All signed the articles, teachers were hired, and the school opened without further delay.

This was in the year 1749. The pupils came in so fast that it was found necessary to find larger quarters for them; and the committee were looking for a place to erect a building upon, when the large structure erected for the Whitfield meetings was suggested to them, and arrangements soon completed for its occupancy. Franklin chanced to be a member of the Board of Trustees for the Church and the Academy both; and he was the more convenient agent for carrying out the transaction. The Church trustees were ready to dispose of the property, because the enthusiasm which was first excited over the project had been by this time far spent, and for the additional reason that they (the trustees) could not raise money enough to pay the ground rent with regularity; and Franklin brought about a cession of the property to the trustees of the new Academy, on condition that the latter should discharge this debt, and likewise keep open in the building a hall for occasional preachers, as was the original intention, and, furthermore, support *a free school* for the instruction of poor children.

The property changed hands with this understanding, and the great building at once underwent many changes. The high hall was converted into stories, and rooms were constructed, above and below, for the convenience of the scholars. The entire labor came on Franklin's shoulders,—buying materials, agreeing with the workmen, and overseeing the operations. But he got through it successfully, and the scholars were all moved in.

He was arrived at a condition of decided prosperity by this time, and could well give his time to public business of this sort. Only the year before he had taken a capable and trusty partner, David Hall by name, who had already been in his employ for four years; and he found, by this new arrangement, that all the business was taken off his hands, Mr. Hall assuming full charge of the printing-office and paying him over his share of the profits of the establishment. They went on together in this manner for eighteen years, and success attended them through the whole of that long term. With the leisure which was now at his disposal, he gave much attention to the interests of the Academy. A charter of incorporation was obtained from the Governor, and land was ceded by the Proprietaries of the province, and money contributed by friends in England; the Assembly also gave its aid, and in due time this beginning resulted in what is known as the University of Pennsylvania. Franklin continued one of its trustees for forty years; and he lived to see many of its pupils filling important stations and adorning the State to which they owed their birth and education.

He had just begun to feel easy in the assurance that he had now fortune enough to secure to him all the leisure he wanted for the prosecution of his philosophical studies, to which he intended to devote the remainder of his life. He had purchased the apparatus of Dr. Spence, who was come over from England to lecture in Philadelphia, and entered upon his electrical experiments with great enthusiasm. So far, very well: but the public, seeing that he had this leisure on his hands, coveted it of him; they meant to lay hold of his time and talents both, and make them serviceable for the general good.

He was called into almost every branch of public life. By the Governor he was made a Justice of the Peace; the city corporation made him at first a member of the Common Council, and afterwards an Alderman; and the citizens at large elected him to represent them in the Assembly. He was grateful for the last post: for he confessed that he had become tired, long ago, of hearing the debates in his clerk's seat, without the privilege of taking part in them, and he felt that his power and influence would very much expand by the new gift. His ambition, too, was not a little flattered by the election, for he considered that, starting from what he styled his "low beginnings," it was a great thing for him. But, better than all, he was glad to know he was held in such esteem by his countrymen.

After sitting as Justice for a few times, he found that his limited knowledge of law hardly allowed him to act in that capacity, and he accordingly withdrew from it, offering by way of excuse that he was called upon to attend to his duties as a legislator. He took his seat in the House, and his son was appointed Clerk.

In the following year, he was appointed by the House, together with the Speaker, a Commissioner to make a treaty with the Indians at Carlisle. Arriving at that place among them, the Commission ordered that the red men should have not a drop of liquor sold them, as they were very apt to get drunk and to become disorderly. The Indians made sore complaint about it; and, to quiet them, they were told that, if they would keep sober while the treaty was under discussion, they should have plenty of rum afterwards. This agreement was faithfully carried out. But when they got their rum at last, the business having all been finished, they made a famous powwow over it. There were nearly a hundred of them in all,— men, women, and children,—and they lodged in cabins, erected in the form of a square, just outside the town.

The Commissioners heard a wild noise among them in the evening, and walked over to see what was the cause of it. They found their red brethren had kindled a large bonfire in the middle of the square, around which they were dancing, and

yelling, and quarrelling. Men and women were
mixed together, and all were drunk. Franklin
said that "their dark-colored bodies, half-naked,
seen only by the gloomy light of the bonfire, running after and beating one another with fire-
brands, accompanied by their horrid yellings,
formed a scene the most resembling our ideas of
hell that could well be imagined." The Commissioners found they could do nothing with
them, and therefore went back to their lodgings.
About midnight, they were startled by thunder-
ings at their door, which turned out to be the
Indians, come for more rum; but no notice was
taken of them.

They were conscious that they had done wrong,
however, and the next day sent over three of their
oldest counsellors with an apology. The one who
spoke for the others acknowledged their fault, but
he laid it to the rum; and then, wishing to say a
good word for the rum, gave the following ex-
planation:— "The Great Spirit, who made all
things, made everything for some use; and whatever use he designed anything for, that use it
should always be put to. Now, when he made
rum, he said, '*Let this be for the Indians to get
drunk with!*'—and it must be so."

Franklin was appealed to, in the year 1751, to aid in establishing a hospital in Philadelphia, for the reception and cure of poor sick persons, whether they happened to belong to the province or were strangers. A subscription had already been set on foot for it, but thus far little had been accomplished; the plan was a novelty in the country, and few had sufficient confidence in it to give it a start. At length Franklin was approached on the subject. He was told that no public measure could be carried through unless he was at the bottom of it. Everybody who had been addressed upon this hospital scheme, wished to know first *what Franklin thought about it.* People would commit themselves to nothing until they heard from *him.*

So he took hold, and, after his usual method, began by writing brief articles on the subject for the newspapers. The subscriptions increased at once; yet not fast enough to warrant the success of the plan without help from the Assembly. He therefore drew a petition to that body. The country members had no relish for the project; their objection was, that it would only be of service to the city, and that the citizens should defray the expense. They even doubted if the inhabitants of Philadelphia were in favor of the plan themselves; but Franklin assured them they were greatly mistaken, for he had no doubt about raising at least two thousand pounds by voluntary contributions. They were faithless, but he went forward with his plan. The bill of incorporation was drawn with the condition, that when the contributors to the stock should organize and raise two thousand pounds, and satisfy the Speaker of the Assembly that that sum had been raised,—*then* the Speaker was authorized and required to draw on the provincial treasurer for two thousand pounds more, in two yearly payments, "for the founding, building and finishing of the hospital." The money raised by the contributors was to be put at interest, and the income applied to the accommodation of the sick poor in the hospital. On this condition the bill was passed. No difficulty was found in raising the whole sum desired, for every contributor felt that for each pound that he gave the province was to give another.

A handsome building was speedily erected for the hospital, and the project went into practical and successful operation immediately afterward. Franklin said that none of his subsequent "political manœuvres" gave him more pleasure; and

16

none furnished him more readily with excuses for using a little cunning.

Next came to him a clergyman with a request that he would help him in getting up a subscription for building a new meeting-house. He at once refused; he was not willing to make himself disagreeable to his fellow-citizens by dunning them for alms. The clergyman then wished him to furnish him with a list of the names of the most generous and willing givers! But Franklin thought—and thought correctly—that a man's generosity should not make him an object to be worried by beggars, and he refused. Finally, seeing he could get no more, the man asked him for his advice. "That I will give you," answered Franklin. "In the first place, I advise you to apply to all those who you know will give something; next, to those who you are uncertain whether they will give anything or not, and show them the list of those who have given; and lastly, do not neglect those who you are sure will give nothing, for in some of them you may be mistaken." The man laughed, thanked him, and promised to do as he bade him. He very soon raised a large sum from his beggings, and a handsome church was erected by the means.

The next public matter which urged itself upon his attention was the condition of the streets. His mind was active respecting everything that concerned the great body of his fellow-citizens. The streets of Philadelphia were laid at right-angles, giving the whole city a beautiful regularity. But they had never been paved, and in wet weather were difficult to traverse with carriages, owing to the thickness of the mud. Living himself near Jersey market, he had noticed with much uneasiness that the people frequenting the place, to purchase provisions, were obliged to stand in the mud; but while standing or walking inside the market, where was a long strip of brick pavement, they were at once dry and comfortable.

Seeing what accumulations were brought to the pavement from the street, he was led to hire a poor man to sweep it twice each week, sweeping the dirt from before the neighbors' doors likewise, paying him sixpence a month for each house. Once more he had resort to writing and printing, and placed in each house a paper, setting forth the advantages of this outside cleanliness; and in a few days he went around to see how many persons would subscribe to an agreement to pay these sixpences for sweeping. The greater part of those called on agreed to the plan, and the pavement around their houses was kept so clean as to attract the attention of the people of the city at large. Out of this little manœuvre sprang a scheme to pave the whole city, for which the inhabitants were very willing to be taxed.

Franklin drew up a bill for that purpose, just before he went to England, in 1757, and introduced it into the Assembly. It was not passed, however, until after he had left, and then with alterations; but one of them was a proposal to light the streets, as well as to pave them. The lighting was done by an individual, who placed a lamp above his own door that the people might see for themselves the advantage of the plan. They were at that time supplied with globe lamps from London; but Franklin subsequently improved the form of them. His improvement consisted in making the lamps with four flat panes, with a long funnel to draw up the smoke, and holes at the bottom to admit the air for draught. They were thus kept clean, and continued bright till morning, not clouding up with smoke in a few hours like the London lamps; and if they were broken, only a single pane had to be replaced, instead of an entirely new lamp.

In this, and in other ways, Franklin made himself continually useful to his fellow-citizens. He would see them surrounded with as many comforts as providence could secure; and to that end his observation was always awake, and his faculties on the alert to second such suggestions as occurred to him. He looked after the streets, the pavements, the lamps, the public institutions; the inhabitants felt that they had a willing servant in so excellent a citizen. He conducted his experiments in philosophy at the same time, and continually made advancement in his scientific studies. What he had to communicate to the public through his newspaper was given in brief and pithy appeals, each of them stuffed out with an anecdote, or shrewdly wise saying, which moved the popular mind much sooner than if written in the form of a speech or a sermon. No man knew better than Franklin how to turn his talents and his time to practical account.

He had been employed by the Postmaster-Genera. of America, for some time previous to 1753, as his comptroller to regulate the business of a good many offices, and to keep the accounts of the officers always under his eye; and as that officer died in the year just named, Franklin, along with William

16*

Hunter, was appointed by a commission from the Postmaster-General of England to succeed him. Up to that time, the American office had never paid a pound of revenue into the general office of the parent country; and, to pay the new appointees their salary, they were to be allowed six hundred pounds a year between them, provided the office would yield that amount of profits.

To bring about a remunerative state of things, they were obliged to resort to many expedients. They were forced to make improvements of every sort, and the first cost of the same was so great that they were out of pocket by it, at the end of the first four years, to the amount of more than nine hundred pounds. After that, however, the money began to come in; and during the time Franklin administered its affairs, it was made to pay three times as much revenue to the Crown as the post-office of Ireland.

His business in connection with the post-office sent him forth on various journeys. That very year he travelled to New England, and was honored with the title of Master of Arts by Harvard University. But Yale College, in New Haven, had been before Harvard with a similar merited compliment. In this way, he says, "without studying

in any college, I came to partake of their honors."
They were conferred on him for his discoveries in
electricity, and his additions to that branch of
natural philosophy.

His philosophical reputation took its rise from
an accidental meeting in Boston, in the year
1746, with a Dr. Spence from Scotland, who had
brought over with him certain instruments with
the design of lecturing and experimenting on
electricity. This man was not very expert at his
business, yet what Franklin saw was sufficient to
surprise and delight him. Not long after he returned to Philadelphia, their library association
received a glass tube as a present from Mr. Peter
Collinson, of London, Fellow of the Royal Society,
with an account of the manner of using it for experiments of that character. Franklin eagerly
improved the opportunity offered to repeat what
had so pleased him, in Boston; and after much
practice, he was able to perform not only what he
had seen there, but likewise those experiments of
which accounts had been written him from England, and to originate several new ones himself.
These electric phenomena were the wonder of the
day; his house was continually thronged with

persons, come to see the astonishing things that were performed.

Finding this a little more of a burden than he cared to shoulder alone, he adroitly managed to divide it up among others, and by this means to make more rapid progress with his experiments. He had a number of glass tubes blown at the glass house in Philadelphia, similar to the one sent them from London, and furnished them to his friends. The person who proved most serviceable to him was a neighbor named Kinnersley, who happened to be out of business, and whom Franklin encouraged to make exhibition of the experiments for money. He was an ingenious person withal, and just such an one as would be likely to spread the fame of these wonderful novelties in scientific discovery. Franklin wrote for him a couple of lectures, sketching the experiments with their explanations in order. He had an elegant apparatus constructed for himself, in which all of Franklin's roughly formed machines were neatly made by regular instrument makers. His lectures drew large audiences, and pleased all. He delivered them in all the chief towns and cities of the colonies, and, as Franklin expresses it, "picked up some money." It was found that in the West

India Islands, however, owing to the moisture of the atmosphere, the experiments could be made only with much difficulty.

The next thing done by Franklin and his little knot of scientific students, was to send back word to England, to Mr. Collinson, who had presented them with the tube and an account of its use in producing electrical phenomena, the result thus far of their doings. Accordingly, Franklin wrote him several letters, filled with recitals of their experiments at Philadelphia. Mr. Collinson procured them to be read before the Royal Society; but none of the members of that *very* learned body thought them of importance, or even of interest, sufficient to merit publication in their regular "Transactions." There was one paper, in particular, that caused actual mirth among those connoisseurs in science : it was one which Franklin had drawn up for Mr. Kinnersley, his neighbor and the lecturer, in which he maintained that electricity was the same thing with lightning. Franklin had sent a copy of it to a friend of his in London, who was a member of the Royal Society; all the response he was able to get respecting it was that it had been read before the members and laughed down.

When Dr. Fothergill read these American accounts, however, he saw, as by instinct, the great value of them, and advised to their printing. Mr. Collinson then handed them to Cave, to be published in the Gentleman's Magazine; but it was thought best by him to put them forth in a distinct pamphlet, to which Dr. Fothergill wrote the preface. The additions which were afterwards added to this first account swelled the pamphlet to the size of a quarto volume, which passed through many editions.

These discoveries, however, failed to attract much attention in England for a long time, owing, no doubt, to the neglect they received at the hands of the Royal Society; but a copy of the pamphlet, with its additions, happened to fall into the hands of Count Buffon, a philosopher of great fame not only in France but throughout Europe, who prevailed on M. Dubourg to translate them into French, and to have the whole printed in Paris. The Abbé Nollet was the preceptor in natural philosophy to the royal family, and had made many experiments in reference to electricity, which were the basis of a theory then generally accepted. To such a person Franklin's startling discoveries were, of course, not at all acceptable, since they tended to overthrow his whole theory and impair his reputation with the public as a philosopher. He was actually *offended* at the publication of Franklin's pamphlet. He would not believe that any experiments of the sort had ever been made in America, but preferred to think that his enemies at Paris had fabricated these accounts on purpose to oppose his system. But being assured, some time afterward, that there really was such a person at Philadelphia as Benjamin Franklin, and that he had made these experiments and discoveries relative to electricity, he wrote and printed a series of letters for the public eye, but ostensibly addressed to Franklin, in which he defended his own theory of electricity, denied the truth of Franklin's experiments, and scouted the inferences which the latter drew from them.

Franklin at one time thought of writing and publishing a reply to this volume of the Abbé's; but, on reflection, it occurred to him that, at best, it would be but a war of *words*, while the *facts*, as set down in his pamphlet, would speak for themselves. If these facts could not be verified, on one side of the Atlantic as well as the other, then they could not be defended; the only way would be, to keep on multiplying the facts, and let them

make their own way. Besides, even having the
advantage of truth on his side, he felt sure that a
controversy carried on in two different languages
was liable to much looseness, and the chances
therefore were that it would end in dissatisfaction
to themselves and disgust to the public. He went
on with his experiments, therefore, instead of
spending his time in unprofitable discussion, and
in this respect proved the wisdom of which he was
really possessed.

His silence never caused him regret. It was not
necessary for him to defend his book, or to come
to the rescue of his facts. The volume was soon
translated into the Italian, German, and Latin
languages, and its doctrines were gradually adopted
by the philosophers of Europe, in preference to
those held by the Abbé Nollet. M. Le Roy, a
friend of Franklin, and a member of the Royal
Academy of Sciences, of France, took up the pen
in defence of the new discoveries and theories
of the latter, completely refuting the Abbé, and
rendering any further attention at Franklin's
hands unnecessary.

There was one thing that helped to bring the
book of Franklin into immediate notice, and to
give it even celebrity; that was the brilliant suc-

cess of one of the experiments which were set
down in it, which was tried by Messieurs De Lor
and Dalibard, at Marly, for drawing down lightning from the clouds. So bold an experiment,
and one unheard of before, challenged the pro-
foundest curiosity of scientific men and excited
the unbounded admiration of all who heard of it.
Nothing was talked of, at the time, but this one
absorbing matter. M. De Lor likewise had an
apparatus for trying philosophical experiments,
and was in the habit of lecturing. In his lectures
on Electricity, he undertook to repeat what then
went by the name of the "Philadelphia Experiments." When once they had been performed in
the presence of the French King and his Court,
all Paris flocked afterwards to witness them.

The experiment of drawing down the lightnings
from the heavens, which was to demonstrate that
they and electricity were one and the same sub-
stance, it was ordained that Franklin should make,
with the simple means which were at his command;
and the story of it belongs in this very place. He
had gone far enough to be assured that in many
points they closely resembled one another; one
final test only remained to be made.

What attracts us more than all to his character,

too, in spite of what flippant modern writers say
of his *penurious maxims* and *saving habits*, is the
perfect openness of it, lying exposed, as it did, to
the advantage or the criticism of all.   He kept no
part of it selfishly in reserve.   While he was conducting the great experiment to which we allude,
he never sought to shut out the light that had
already reached him from the eyes of other in-
quirers, but published his ideas as fast as they
occurred to him, and freely invited all other
students of philosophy to pursue the same object
with himself.

His original plan for drawing the electric fluid
from the clouds was by raising insulated bars of
iron to great heights in the air.   On this hint, the
experimenters in England and France practised
with metallic bars, but nothing decisive came of
it.   At length the true mode occurred to him.
Like all of the grand discoveries of the age, it
was effected through the simplest means.   He
made a kite of silk, choosing that rather than
paper because the rain would not harm it, to which
he fixed a slender barb, or point, of iron.   The
string by which the kite was held was also of silk,
and at the end of the string, just below his hand,
hung a key.

With so simple an instrument as this, he went out into the suburbs of Philadelphia one day when a thunder storm was coming over the town, and set his kite flying toward the clouds. What great results, in the line of discoveries, hung on that single little experiment! The lightning in the clouds soon caught his point of iron at the head of the kite, and, traversing the kite, found its swift way along the rudely constructed silken string. He could himself see that the fibres of silk were raised by the subtle contact. Now came the moment of his great anxiety and his triumph. Applying his knuckle to the key which hung from the end of the string, he drew from it a living spark! Again and again he did so, and each time with similar success. He then charged a vial which he had at hand with the fluid, drawing it from the clouds through the key, and found it would explode gunpowder, set spirits of wine on fire, and perform all other tricks which were performed by electricity itself.

The experiment was a success. The printer-philosopher had made a discovery from which consequences of the most important character were to be secured to the human family. His pleasure it is no part of our task to attempt to describe.

To this account of his great experiment with the kite should be added a recital of some of the various little electrical amusements with which he relaxed his mind in the intervals of his severer studies, and entertained the friends who were in the habit of frequenting his house. One of these was "the Magic Pistol," an instrument which he charged with inflammable air, stopped with a cork, and fired by means of a charged rod near the pistol's mouth. On drawing the rod, the electric spark flew in, and the inflammable air was set on fire. Out went the cork with a sharp report, hitting any object against which it might be aimed.

Another was a set of toys, composed of little dogs made of elder pith, with straw feet and tails. He would place these little fellows upon the table, and, taking a large tumbler, or receiver, which had been charged with the fluid, clapped it suddenly over them. Upon this they all began to dance and skip about, and to make attempts to run up the sides of the glass, as if to get out. These Franklin used to call his "dancing dogs."

Still another was a plate of tin, cut into the form of a star, and secure to the end of a prime conductor. On putting out the candles, and making a turn or two of the jar, the fluid danced and shimmered at all the angles of the cut tin-plate, and made a light as beautiful as it is possible to conceive. He called this toy "the electric star."

Another was more ingenious than the foregoing, and intended to illustrate a well-known Scripture story. He had a large picture of a man dressed in purple and fine linen, and behind it stood concealed an electrical jar. A little way off was a small brass pillar, and by it lay a ragged beggar. Suspended from the ceiling, and reaching down to the table on which stood the jar, was the picture of a boy, beautiful, and of an angelic expression. The picture of the man who was dressed in purple and fine linen he called Dives; while that of the beautiful boy he named the Son of Dives; the poor man reclining at the base of the post he called Lazarus. His trick was to make Dives, who had in his imaginary lifetime refused to help Lazarus, now administer comfort and aid to him through his son. In order to do this, he charged the concealed jar with electricity. This drew the youth to it, who, on being charged with the fluid, flew in great haste to the brass pillar at the foot of which

17*

lay Lazarus, and there discharged his whole burden. On being thus relieved, he once more hastened back to the jar behind Dives,—although to the spectator he only appeared to approach Dives himself,—where he got his second load, which he emptied at the feet of Lazarus as before. After he had equalized the quantity of electric fluid between them, by thus taking from one and giving to the other, he rested satisfied. This toy he named "Dives and Lazarus."

The Royal Society of London by this time took up the serious consideration of the letters he had some time before sent over to them, but which had been until then superciliously neglected. They felt obliged to do so from very shame, in order to keep abreast with the new discoveries; the Paris Society had received and considered them with enthusiasm, and its London associate was forced to do what it had so long and so ignorantly refused to do.

They paid Franklin the compliment of choosing him a member; excused him from paying the customary fees; and presented him with the Copley gold medal for 1753, which was accompanied with a highly complimentary speech by the President of the Society, Lord Macclesfield.

CHAPTER IX.

AS A MILITARY MAN.

THE lords of trade in the mother country sent over orders, in 1754, that a Congress of Commissioners from the several colonies should be held at Albany, to confer with the chiefs of the Six Nations, Indian tribes in central and western New York, about the defence of the country of both peoples against the expected invasion of France. War with France was just then apprehended by Great Britain, which afterwards did break out, and became a protracted contest on this side of the Atlantic for the possession of the continent. It lasted some seven years, and is known in history as the old French and Indian War.

The Governor of Pennsylvania named four persons to constitute the commission for that colony, among whom was Benjamin Franklin. They took with them presents for the Indians, and met with the commissioners from the other colonies, at Albany, about the middle of June. They stopped in New York on their way to Albany, and Franklin laid before two gentlemen of wide experience in public affairs in that city—Mr. James Alexander and Mr. Kennedy,—a plan which he had devised for an *Union of all the colonies under one government*, for the common defence and other purposes. This was, in fact, the quiet suggestion which proved the forerunner of the great federative movement made twenty years later. It seemed as if there then lay in Franklin's brain the germ of the scheme which was to secure the independence of the colonies.

On reaching Albany, his plan for an union having met the approbation of the two gentlemen named, he lost no time in presenting it to the Congress. He found that other commissioners had likewise projected plans of a similar character. The first step taken, therefore, was to put it to a vote whether such an union should be formed; and it was decided in the affirmative without a dissenting vote. Upon this, a committee of one from each colony was raised, to consider the several plans which were brought in, and duly report upon them. The committee gave Franklin's plan the preference over the others, and reported it back to the Congress with a few amendments. As this plan of union is become an important matter in our history as a nation, room may be claimed here for a statement of its features, and its history.

In the first place, the general government of the colonies thus united was to be administered by a President-General, who should receive his appointment and support from England. Next, a grand Council was to be elected by the colonial assemblies, which were the direct representatives of the people. The Congress took it up and debated it, at the same time that the Indian business was under discussion. All the objections possible to raise against it were brought up, discussed, and finally removed; and at length the scheme was adopted by the body of commissioners, and copies of it were ordered to be sent to the Board of Trade in London, as well as to the Assemblies of the various colonies.

The assemblies refused to adopt it, because they thought it gave too much power over colonial affairs to the crown; while the English government refused its sanction to the measure, because it deemed the scheme much too *democratic*, leaving more power in the hands of the people of the colonies than was consistent with the supreme control of the mother

government. It was not adopted by the Board of
Trade, nor did that body recommend it to the favor
of the king. But in place of it, they projected
another scheme, which they professed to believe a
much better one. It was as follows :—that the
Governors of the provinces, together with a stated
number of members of their Councils, should
meet whenever they thought best, and order troops
to be raised, forts to be built, and draw on the
treasury of Great Britain for money to defray the
expense; and the money thus drawn from the
English treasury was to be paid back again by a
tax laid by Parliament on the American provinces.

In the winter of 1754–5, Franklin was in Boston,
and exchanged views often with Governor Shirley
on the plans both of the Congress and of Great
Britain. The letters which passed between them
form a part of the most interesting history of that
important period. Franklin was always inclined
to believe that his proposed plan was the safe and
proper one, because it was so strongly liked and
opposed. He thought it would have been better
for the country if it had then been adopted; for
the colonies, united in this way, would have been
strong enough to take care of themselves; there
would have been no need of bringing over troops

from England; and, in that way, the pretext which was afterwards raised in Great Britain for taxing the colonies could never have existed,— and the long and weary war which ensued in consequence of the tax, would have been wholly avoided. But, says Franklin, moralizing on this point, "the best public measures are seldom adopted from previous wisdom, but forced by the occasion." The plan of union, as proposed by Franklin, met with the approbation of the Governor of Pennsylvania, however, who spoke of it "as appearing to be drawn up with great clearness and strength of judgment;" and he recommended it to the Assembly "as well worthy of their closest and most serious attention." But in Franklin's absence, it was unfairly brought up by a member, who, by artful management, procured it to be condemned by the House.

Stopping in New York on his way to Boston, he met there the newly appointed Pennsylvania Governor, just come over from Europe,—Governor Morris, with whom he had had a previous familiar acquaintance. Governor Hamilton had resigned his office, tired of the disputes that were set agoing by his instructions from the Proprietors, who resided in England. Governor Morris asked Franklin if he might anticipate for himself as unquiet and troublesome an administration. "No," said the latter; "you may, on the contrary, have a very comfortable one, if you will only take care not to enter into any dispute with the Assembly." "My dear friend," was the reply of Morris, "how can you advise my avoiding disputes? You know I love disputing; it is one of my greatest pleasures. However, to show the regard I have for your counsel, I promise you I will, if possible, avoid them." And on this general practice of disputation, let us here quote the words of so wise a man as Dr. Franklin. He says that Morris "had some *reason* for loving to dispute, being eloquent, an acute sophister, and therefore generally successful in argumentative conversation. He had been brought up to it from a boy, his father, as I have heard, accustoming his children to dispute with one another for his diversion while sitting at table after dinner; but I think the practice *was not wise*, for, in the course of my observation, those disputing, contradicting, and confuting people are generally unfortunate in their affairs. They get victory sometimes, but they never get good will, which would be of more use to them."

Gov. Morris soon got into disputes with the As-

sembly, however, in spite of his promises to Franklin. The latter heard of it, as soon as he reached
New York on his way home. After he got back,
he took his own seat in the Assembly, and was
straightway placed on every committee which was
appointed for drawing up replies to the Governor's
messages and speeches. Both the messages and
the replies were, as Franklin confesses, "often
tart, and sometimes *indecently abusive;*" and inasmuch as the Governor knew very well who drew
them up, it would have been natural to expect
that when they met they would have flown at one
another's throats. Such was by no means the
case, however; on the contrary, they often dined
together. The Governor was personally one of
the best natured of men.

While this public quarrel was at its height, they
met one day in the street. Said the Governor—
"Franklin, you must go home with me and spend
the evening; I am to have some company that you
will like." And he took him by the arm, and led
him to his house. Over their wine, after supper,
while indulging in a strain of frolicsome talk, the
Governor said that he was much taken with Sancho
Panza's idea, who replied, when he was told that
a government was about to be given to him, that

18

he hoped it would be a government of blacks; for then, if he could not *agree* with his people, he could *sell* them. One of the Governor's friends, who sat next Franklin at the table, said to him— "Franklin, why do you continue to side with those damned Quakers? Had you not better sell them? the Proprietor would give you a good price." Franklin replied—"The Governor has not yet *blacked* them enough." And the latter went on to comment, that he had indeed labored hard to blacken the Assembly in all his messages, but they wiped off his coloring as fast as he laid it on, and placed it thick on his own face, in return; so that, finding he was in a way of being *negrofied* himself, he grew sick of his government and quitted the province.

Now that war was really at their doors, the Massachusetts Bay Colony projected an expedition against Crown Point; and in order to secure aid and co-operation, they sent Mr. Quincy to Pennsylvania, and Mr. Pownall, who was afterward Governor, to New York. Franklin being in the Assembly, and being a native of the same colony with Mr. Quincy, he was able to do a good deal for him. The latter applied to him at once for advice and assistance. Franklin helped him to draw up an address to the Assembly, and it was well received by that body. They voted ten thousand pounds in aid of the expedition, the money to be laid out in provisions. But the Governor refused his signature to the bill, unless the estates of the Proprietaries were exempted from taxation. This Proprietary interest and influence will be explained shortly. Mr. Quincy tried hard to induce the Governor to assent to the bill, but to no purpose. Franklin then devised a plan for getting along without him; which was, by orders on the Loan Office, which the Assembly had a legal right to draw. Just then, there happened to be no money in the office; and Franklin proposed that the orders should be payable in a year, at five per cent. interest.

This was at once adopted by the Assembly. These orders were very rapidly taken up by persons having money to invest; for their money was at once put upon interest; and the printed orders which they held were as readily passed from hand to hand as if they had been bank notes. And so the aid for which Mr. Quincy had come from Massachusetts was all rendered at last, and he went back with a heart full of joy to his own people. Before going, however, he returned thanks to the

House in a handsomely written address. He ever
after entertained for Franklin the sincerest friendship.

War having broken out, and Great Britain having refused to countenance the union of the colo
nies, of course the government was obliged to send
over here the troops which it would not permit
the colonies to raise among themselves. The
famous General Braddock was therefore shipped
to America, with a couple of regiments of English
troops. He landed at Alexandria, in Virginia,
and marched with his force from that place to
Fredericktown, in Maryland. Both places have
become very well known to all readers since the
war of the Great Rebellion, in this country. The
Pennsylvania Assembly feared that he, or his masters, had conceived a strong prejudice against
them, and sent off Franklin to meet and confer
with him; not as an authorized agent of theirs,
but rather as Postmaster-General of the colonies,
professing to desire an arrangement with him for
the best mode of sending intelligence from the
army to the several Governors with the greatest
despatch. Franklin was to assume that he would
require to have a correspondence with them, and

the expense of it they of course proposed to pay themselves.

He set out, therefore, with his son in company, and met General Braddock at Fredericktown, waiting for the wagons to come in for which he had sent around among the settlers in the back parts of Maryland and Virginia. He was with the General several days; dined with him; and improved the time to remove his prejudices by acquainting him with what the Assembly had done before he and his troops arrived, and what they were still willing to do to advance his plans. Just as Franklin was about to depart, the wagons came in to headquarters. There were but twenty-five of them in all, and not every one of those was worth anything for his purpose. So great was the General's astonishment, he declared that nothing could be done, and that the expedition would have to be abandoned. His officers were of the same opinion. They could not get along with less than one hundred and fifty wagons; and it was very natural for them to blame their government for sending them into a country where no transportation was provided them.

Franklin said to the officers that he wished they had been landed in Pennsylvania, because in that

18*

country nearly every farmer had his wagon. Braddock seized hold of the suggestion at once. "Then you," said he to Franklin, "who are a man of influence there, can probably procure them for us; and I beg you will undertake it." The terms were talked of between them. Franklin stated them on paper. They were at once agreed to. He posted to Lancaster, and published them there as an advertisement. The effect was direct. In this advertisement, he told the people that one hundred and fifty four-horse wagons, and fifteen hundred saddle, or pack, horses were wanted; and that he should be at Lancaster and York for stated periods, to agree with them for said wagons and teams, on terms which he announced,—the wagons to earn so many shillings per day, the horses so many, and the pay for seven days to be given in advance.

Thus was Franklin become an army contractor. He authorized his son William to enter into similar contracts in an adjoining county.

In addition to this advertisement, he issued to the inhabitants of York, Lancaster, and Cumberland an address, setting forth the condition of affairs with the army at Frederick, informing them that it nad been the intention of Gen. Braddock to send out parties of soldiers to take from the farmers by force the wagons and horses which were wanted, and appealing to them by every consideration to come forward and show their loyalty for their own government and country. "The King's business," said he, "must be done. So many brave troops, come so far for your defence, must not stand idle through your backwardness to do what may be reasonably expected from you. Wagons and horses must be had. Violent measures will probably be used; and you will be left to seek a recompense where you can find it, and your case, perhaps, be little pitied or regarded." He further told them that he was obliged to send the General word of his success within fourteen days; and if they did not come promptly to the rescue, a body of soldiers would immediately enter the province to go about the work of impressment.

He received eight hundred pounds of General Braddock to make purchases with, and advanced two hundred himself; and in two weeks, wagons and horses were on their way to the camp. The farmers, knowing nothing of Gen. Braddock, insisted that Franklin should sign the bonds for the performance of the contract; which he did.

Franklin likewise got up a subscription in the Assembly for the officers in this expedition through the wilderness, and furnished them with twenty parcels of comforts, which were packed upon as many horses, each parcel being intended as a present for every officer, and containing a stated quantity of sugar, tea, coffee, chocolate, vinegar, cheese, butter, wine, spirits, hams, tongue, and so forth. They felt very grateful to him, and the Colonels of both regiments expressed to him the thanks of the officers under them. Gen. Braddock was also pleased with Franklin's prompt agency in getting him wagons, and paid his accounts without delay. Franklin was busily employed in forwarding supplies to his army, according to request, until the news came of his most unexpected defeat; at that time he had advanced of his own money, for provisions, fully a thousand pounds. Luckily, as he admits, the bills were paid before the disaster, with the exception of a small remainder; that he never got.

Franklin thought Braddock a brave man, as did every one who knew him; but he held too high notions about the valor of British regulars on the one hand, and too mean ones of Americans and Indians on the other. An Indian interpreter joined him on his march against Fort Duquesne, with a body of a hundred Indians, who might have been of great use to him as guides and scouts; but he paid but little attention to them, thinking their services of no value, and they quietly left him and his army to their fate. He told Franklin, one day, what he intended to do, as confident in his feelings as if he could walk over the continent unmolested. Said he, "after taking Fort Duquesne, I am to proceed to Niagara; and, having taken that, to Frontenac, if the season will allow time, and I suppose it will; for Duquesne can hardly detain me above three or four days; and then I see nothing that can obstruct my march to Niagara." Franklin was not so sanguine; and pointed out to him the danger to be apprehended from ambuscades in the wilderness, and the liability to his long column of being cut into many parts by the Indians before one part could come to the relief of the other. But Braddock smiled at Franklin's ignorance, answering him that "these savages might strike dread in the hearts of the *American militia*, but never would move the disciplined troops of *Britain*." How dearly he paid for his boasting! Franklin was sure of his own opinion, yet did not feel qualified to combat that of an experienced military man; so he said nothing more.

The story of Braddock's expedition against Fort Duquesne must be told here in few words. He had pushed on through the wilderness, his troops cutting their narrow roads in some places as they went, until they came within about nine miles of the place. A part of the army had crossed a river, and waited until the other part came over; this brought them all in one body, and in an open place in the wilderness: and *then* the enemy opened on them with a murderous fire from an ambuscade, every bush, tree, log, and rock concealing an unerring marksman. Until this deadly fire was opened, General Braddock had no idea that the foe were anywhere near him.

The guard was instantly thrown into disorder, and the troops were hurried forward to their relief, making their way precipitately among the crowded wagons, baggage, and horses. Then a fire as suddenly broke forth upon their flank. The officers formed very conspicuous marks for the fire of the secreted foe, because they were on horseback; and they fell to the ground as fast as they could be sighted by the enemy. The troops were huddled together in a body, and heard no orders from their officers; all they did, therefore, was to stand still and be shot down. In this way, fully two-thirds of them were slaughtered. They afterwards—what were left of them—were struck with a panic, and fled in great terror. The drivers took a horse apiece from their teams, mounted, and rode hastily away; and thus all the wagons, artillery, stores, and provisions were left behind for the enemy.

General Braddock was wounded, and brought away after much trouble and risk. His secretary was killed at his side; and out of eighty-six officers sixty-three were killed and wounded. Out of the eleven hundred men who had been picked from the whole army and sent forward,—the remainder having been left behind to follow with the heavier portion of the stores, provisions, and baggage,—seven hundred and fourteen were killed! The survivors fled back to the camp, and communicating the panic, hastened along until they reached the towns and cities of the settlements again. The enemy did not all together exceed four hundred, of French and Indians; yet the whole body of the English troops fled in affright, though they numbered over a thousand. They ought to have hurried back, and tried to recover

their lost advantages; instead of that, all the remaining stores were destroyed by them where they
were, and the troops went on, in spite of the requests of the Governors of Maryland, Virginia,
and Pennsylvania that they should post themselves
on the frontiers, not resting until the officers
arrived safely in Philadelphia. The Americans
had a much smaller opinion of the British regulars,
after that, than even the regulars had of them.

General Braddock, after being brought off the
field, was entirely silent the first day, and did not
speak until night; then he said—" Who would
have thought it?" All the next day, too, he was
speechless; and at the last he merely said—" We
shall know how to deal with them another time,"—
and died a few minutes after.

The owners of the wagons and horses, as soon
as it was known that all were lost, came upon
Franklin for their value, although the same were
only *hired*, not bought, for the use of the army.
He had a good deal of trouble with them, and was
much perplexed with lawsuits. Commissioners
were, after a time, appointed to examine the
accounts, and to pay them. Had Franklin
been forced to pay them, it would have ruined
him.

Some persons in Philadelphia tried to get up a plan for a grand display of fireworks, to be let off as soon as the capture of Fort Duquesne should be made known. Franklin dissuaded them from it, for reasons which he gave them, and saved them from much mortification.

Franklin was very active, at this time and subsequently, in organizing a volunteer militia, and had carried a bill in aid of the measure through the House, leaving the Quakers at liberty to enlist or not. He wrote an imaginary dialogue on the matter, bringing forward all the objections he could to the measure, and answering them again.

The Governor, Morris, prevailed on him to take charge of the northwest frontier, where the enemy swarmed in great numbers, and to construct a line of forts there, and raise a sufficient number of troops. He soon got together between five and six hundred men. His son was his aid-de-camp, who had served in the preceding war against Canada, and by his experience in the field was of great use to his father. The Indians had burned a Moravian village, called Guadenhutten, and slaughtered all the inhabitants; but as it was thought to be a good place for erecting one of his

19

forts, he assembled his companies at Bethlehem, which was the chief settlement of the Moravians, designing to march thither. The people of that village were all in arms, and ready for the Indians. They helped Franklin in getting off his expedition, supplying him with wagons, stores, and cattle.

He divided his force into three parts, sending one to the upper, and another to the lower waters of the Minisink, while he went himself with the third to Guadenhutten. He had marched but a few miles, when a rain set in. There were no houses for a long distance, and they found no shelter until they came to the barn of a German farmer, into which they all huddled, tired and thoroughly wet. They could not have defended themselves with any effectiveness had they been attacked; for their guns were good for but little, and the men could not keep the locks dry, either. A party of eleven farmers who had borrowed guns of them to go back and recover cattle which the Indians had stolen, were killed with one exception. The one who escaped came back and told that they could not fire off their guns, because the priming was wet.

They reached Guadenhutten the next day, and

constructed a hut for shelter, the first thing. They did not carry tents, as troops on the march do now. They next buried the dead farmers, their bodies not having been properly interred by the frightened people of the settlement. On the next morning the fort was planned and marked out. It was to be four hundred and fifty-five feet in circumference, and defended with palisades, each a foot in diameter. The men fell to chopping trees for this purpose with great zeal. A pine of fourteen inches in diameter two men would fell in six minutes. A trench was dug all around the fort, three feet deep, into which the palisades were planted. They took the wagon-bodies from the wheels, and used the latter to draw the palisades from the woods; each wagon thus furnishing four wheels, they had twice as many carriages as they otherwise would.

The palisades were set up strongly, and a platform erected all around them for the garrison to stand upon and fire at the Indians through the loop-holes. A swivel was mounted, which they discharged forthwith, to let the savages know what they might expect if they came too near. The fort was completed in a week, although it rained hard every other day. The men were kept so close at work, they had no time to be discontented. This reminded Franklin of an old sea captain, who gave orders, when his hands were out of work, that they should *scour the anchor*.

By-and-bye, they took courage from seeing no Indians, and made excursions for some distance outside. They found where the Indians had concealed themselves to watch their proceedings, on the neighboring hills. Franklin speaks of the ingenuity of the Indians in building their fires so as to keep their feet warm, yet so as not to betray themselves to the people in the fort.

His chaplain complained to him that the men could not be made to attend prayers daily. As a gill of rum was furnished them with their regular rations, Franklin advised him to give out that the rum would be distributed right after prayers. He acted on the advice, and had no more trouble with inattention to worship. Hardly had Franklin got the fort stored with provisions when the Governor summoned him home to attend a session of the Assembly. His friends also wrote pressing letters for his return. He had completed three forts, and, as the people of the region were contented to remain on their farms under protection of these forts, he resolved to return. Colonel Clapham, of

New England, took command, and Franklin gave him a commission. The soldiers escorted him back as far as Bethlehem, where he slept in a bed for the first time since he had been gone. He said he could hardly go to sleep, the first night, it was so different from his hard lodging on the floor of a hut, with only a blanket or two. He made many inquiries about the customs of the Moravians, during the few days he stayed at Bethlehem, showing that his active mind was ever awake to the acquisition of knowledge.

When he got back to Philadelphia, he found the volunteer soldiery movement going on as well as he could have wished. The officers of the several companies met and elected Franklin their Colonel, which office he accepted, this time. Thus he became, for a brief period, Colonel Franklin. He was at the head of about twelve hundred men, including a company of artillerymen with six brass field pieces; they had become so expert as to be able to fire them at the rate of twelve times a minute. When Colonel Franklin reviewed his regiment for the first time, they marched with him to the door of his house, and insisted on firing a salute in his honor. The discharges knocked down several pieces of his delicate electrical appa-

19*

ratus; and he moralized, upon this occurrence, that his newly found honors were scarcely less brittle. He had occasion to make a journey into Virginia, soon after, and the officers of his regiment took it into their heads that it would be a good idea to escort their Colonel out of town. Thirty or forty of them, in uniform and on horseback, rode up to his door just as he was about getting upon his own horse, astonishing him with their appearance. He felt a little "flat" when he saw what they would do, but could not stop them. Some busybody wrote an account of it to the Proprietor, who felt exceedingly wroth over it, declaring that no such honor had ever been paid to himself while in the province, nor even to the Governor; and that it was due to no less a person than the prince royal. A great deal of bad blood was excited against Franklin in the heart of the Proprietor, who brought charges against him before the ministry, and, among them, that he alone stood in the way of the king's service in Pennsylvania. He likewise tried to influence the Postmaster-General to deprive him of his office.

The Governor seriously proposed to Franklin that he should set out with a second expedition against Fort Duquesne, after Braddock's defeat, and would have commissioned him a General; but Franklin had a poor opinion of his own military abilities, and did not accept an offer with which so many men would feel flattered. He thought he knew better of his own capacities than the Governor could know for him.

CHAPTER X.

FIRST FIVE YEARS IN EUROPE.

WHEN Governor Denny, the new Governor, came over from England, he brought with him the medal which the Royal Society had voted to present Franklin, and bestowed it on him at a public entertainment which the city gave the Governor by way of welcome. He told Franklin in private that he had been urged in London to make his acquaintance on his arrival, and to seek his advice. And he had much to say to him about cultivating harmony between the Proprietor and the Province, hoping that all former disputes with the Assembly would be dropped, and that he would readily lend his own influence to that end. They had this private talk in another room, while the company were at the table; and as they remained a long time, some of those present sent out to them a decanter of

Madeira, which Franklin said the Governor partook liberally of, and piled up promises and pledges as fast as he tossed off bumpers of the wine.

Franklin made answer to his proposals in a spirit of perfect independence; telling him that his means placed him above the necessity of depending on the favors of proprietaries, and that, as a member of the Assembly, he could not accept any such; that he never need fear his opposition to his measures, provided they were calculated to benefit the people; and that he thanked the Governor for his expressions of regard for him, and would do as much as he could to make his administration easy, if he did not bring over with him instructions similar to the odious ones of his predecessor.

On the assemblage of the Legislature, however, owing to the Governor's instructions which he had brought with him from England, a war broke out between him and that body without much delay; and Franklin took an active part in the opposition, as he had done before. Still the Governor and he had no quarrel personally. They often went together, and, as he was both a man of letters and a man of the world, his conversation was pleasing and instructive. Among other items of intelligence which he brought to Franklin, he told him that his old friend Ralph was still living, and that he was then considered one of the best political writers in England ; he had taken part in the dispute between Prince Frederick and the king, and enjoyed a pension of three hundred pounds a year. His fame as a poet, however, was small, and Pope had ridiculed him in the Dunciad; but his prose was as good as any man's.

At this point of time, Franklin appears as the colonial agent—first of Pennsylvania, and afterwards of other colonies,—in England. It was a work that engrossed many of the best years of his life, giving him opportunities for employing his natural talents for diplomacy to the best advantage. All his previous life was but a preparation for this which was to come. He had amassed what might be thought a sufficient fortune, and his fame as a philosopher and discoverer had gone before him over Europe. His experience as a legislator was calculated to stand him in good stead before the parliaments of the old world; while his minute knowledge of colonial affairs, of the conduct and character of the Indians on the frontier, and of the real ability of the men of his own country as material for war, was of the first consequence to him in the turmoil of the events he was summoned to pass through.

Owing to the continued troubles between the Assembly and the proprietaries, and the persistency with which the latter sought to cripple the free action of the people of the province in all matters, the latter determined to petition the king directly against their would-be tyrants, and appointed Franklin their agent to go to England to present the petition. It appears that the House had passed a bill, and sent it to the Governor for his signature, granting sixty thousand pounds for the king's use, and ten thousand of it subject to the orders of Lord Loudoun, then General. The Governor refused absolutely to let the bill become a law.

Franklin engaged his passage to London with Captain Morris, who sailed a packet out of New York, and sent all his stores for the passage on board. A sea voyage was a very different affair, it need not be said, from what it is now. Just as he was leaving, Lord Loudoun arrived in Philadelphia, on purpose to try and bring about a reconciliation between the Assembly and the Governor, so that His Majesty's service might not suffer harm from their differences. He made an appointment for the Governor and himself to meet him on the subject. They came together, and went over the merits of the case. Franklin urged the side he had always taken before the Assembly; while the Governor argued for the binding character of his instructions, and showed that his ruin would follow their disobedience; yet he showed that he *might* consent to disregard them if he could but receive orders to that effect from Lord Loudoun. The latter, however, scarcely dared give his consent, and he finally went so far over to the views of the Governor as to tell Franklin that he would better use all his influence with the Assembly to provide for the defence of the frontier themselves, for, as for himself, he would not consent to spare a single one of the king's troops for that purpose.

The matter was soon after arranged by Franklin between the Assembly and the Governor, and he proceeded on his voyage. But, on arriving in New York, he found that the packet on which he was to go had sailed with all his stores. He thus lost these, receiving in return nothing but the thanks of Loudoun, while the latter took all the credit of the compromise to himself.

Franklin found that Lord Loudoun had gone on to New York before him. He, of course, had control over the sailing of the packets, since he was to send dispatches by them to his government. There were two vessels then in port, one of which he said would sail very soon. Franklin wished him to name the day, so that he might lose as little time as need be. His lordship told him she would sail the Saturday following; but he added, confidentially, that if he should be on board by the Monday morning following, it would be time enough. Franklin was hindered by the ferry, and did not reach the vessel until noon of Monday. When he arrived, what was his surprise to find that she would not sail until the next day!

And so the matter went on, day succeeding day, and still the vessel not ready to depart. It was all owing to the natural indecision of Loudoun's character. Franklin came to New York to take passage about the first of April; it was very near the last of June before he took his departure. The General's letters were always to be ready *to-morrow*, and *to-morrow;* but one packet after another arrived and was detained by his orders, until there were *four* of them waiting to carry his despatches to his government. The merchants

20

were in a fever over the delay, for they had sent
out orders by the vessels for their autumn goods,
which required despatch in order to make their
trade worth any thing to them. They were anxious
about their letters, too, and were subjected to the
payment of heavy rates of insurance besides, it
being war time. But their urgency availed nothing.
Whoever waited on his lordship to see what was
the cause of the delay, found him at his desk,
plunged in the industrious preparation of his
despatches.

All the passengers who were to sail finally went
down to Sandy Hook, where they awaited the
movements of the fleet; there they were compelled
to remain for *six weeks*, using up their sea stores
and being obliged to purchase more. The fleet
set sail at length for Louisburg, with the General
on board, with intent to reduce and capture that
place; he kept the several packet boats dancing
attendance on him all the way, to be ready to take
his despatches when he should have made them
up. In this way he compelled them to hover for
five days around the fleet, and then the ship on
which Franklin was received permission to depart
for England. The other packets were detained
still longer; in fact, he took them down near

Louisburg with him, then changed his mind about attacking the place, and finally turned and went back to New York again. The passengers were incensed to a high degree, and swore all manner of revenge upon him for such treatment.

When Lord Loudoun was first sent over by the ministry to take charge of the war against the French and Indians, and to supersede Gen. Shirley, the citizens of New York gave him an entertainment, at which Shirley was himself present. Franklin was invited to attend likewise. He chanced to be placed near Gen. Shirley, whom he observed to have been seated in a very low chair, the crowd compelling them to send out and borrow chairs. Franklin remarked the fact to the General, saying—"They have given you a very low seat." "No matter, Mr. Franklin," said he, "I find a *low seat* the easiest." Loudoun's foolish flourish before Louisburg, which resulted in nothing, lost the country Fort George, and placed the colonies in a situation of greater danger than before.

The voyage to England proved, after all, to be a pleasant one. Franklin amused himself with computations respecting the speed of the ship, and experimental calculations of the best mode of sailing her; and he afterwards set down his own reflections on the matter, throwing out many a hint which has, since his day, been made much of by builders of ships. Their vessel was several times chased by French privateers during the passage, but they managed to outsail everything of a hostile character. When they arrived off the coast, they came frightfully near being wrecked on the rocks at midnight, owing to the carelessness of the man on the watch; but by the great skill of the captain, who was roused from his sleep below, they wore round the rocks, and went on shore at Falmouth the next forenoon. Franklin had his son with him, and set out forthwith for London, stopping by the way only to see Stonehenge, on Salisbury Plain, and some antiquities at Wilton.

He arrived in London, the accredited agent of the American Colonies, on the 27th of July, 1757. He was in his fifty-second year. Thirty years before, he had landed there under very different circumstances; now he came bringing with him the respect and confidence of all at home, and to be welcomed by a wide European fame, which had gone before him. For his writings and discoveries as a politician and a philosopher, he was most cordially met by statesmen and men of science.

He received attention and respect at the hands of all men. He was already a member of the Royal Society, which was a sufficient passport into the best circles. Peter Collinson, another member of that society, who had been his correspondent for some time in England, invited him to his house, where he remained until he took lodgings a few doors from the Strand, at Mrs. Stevenson's. Some of his Pennsylvania friends had recommended this lady's house to him as an excellent place to board, and he continued there during the whole of his stay in England, which was fifteen years. He became greatly attached to the family, and speaks frequently of them in his letters. Some of his best papers on philosophy were written for the instruction of his landlady's daughter, Miss Mary Stevenson, who early attracted him by her inquiring mind and habits of study.

Among the acquaintances of former days and other places which he renewed in London, was that of Gov. Shirley, once of Massachusetts; they were at once intimate again. But the most of his new friends were among scientific men and philosophers, his taste for politics being kept down by his fondness for studies in philosophy. As soon as his arrival in England was known, letters came

20*

to him from all over the continent, written by men distinguished in the walks of science, testifying their respect and admiration both for himself and his attainments.

His first misfortune, however, after his arrival, was to be prostrated with sickness, which kept him at home for nearly two months. It was occasioned by a cold and a fever, producing much pain in his head, and frequently delirium. Before he could get relief, which was obtained only by cupping and the free use of Peruvian bark, he became so much reduced as to be very low indeed.

When he did get out again, he addressed himself first of all to the business on which he had been sent. He waited on the Proprietaries, and laid before them the instructions with which he came armed from the Pennsylvania Assembly. The former received his statements in a bad temper, refusing to do in any wise differently from what they were now doing by the Governors; they held that they had the right to interpret the colonial charters for themselves, and to send out instructions for the Governors accordingly. Yet they promised to consider the remonstrance he presented Franklin left them without the hope of

making any impression, and settled it in his mind
to appeal very soon to a higher tribunal.

The Proprietaries in question were two sons of
the famous William Penn,—Thomas and Richard
Penn. They were beforehand with Franklin, and
used all their influence to throw obstacles in the
way of his plan. The officers of the Crown, too,
were averse to his design, from fear of a diminution of the prerogative of the Crown; and they
were the ones to whom the whole question was to
be finally submitted. Then there was a latent
prejudice against the Quakers of Pennsylvania for
being so backward with the war, and for even opposing it altogether. The papers took up the
story also, and labored hard to excite all the prejudice possible against his errand.

He waited patiently for an opportunity to stem
the torrent, which was not long in offering. One
of the newspapers reported, as coming through
letters from Philadelphia, that the Assembly was
doing nothing but quarrel with the Governor,
while the Indians swarmed all around on the frontier; and that they would vote no money for relief
except on such conditions that the Governor could
not accept it. In other words, the Quakers were
charged with obstinately standing in the way of

all progress. Franklin sent a letter to the pub-
lisher of the paper, signed by his son, denying the
whole of it; and to show how unfairly he was
treated, he was compelled to pay for the insertion
of the letter, although it just as much belonged
to the printer to give it to the public as to have
published the original charges. That letter shed
a new light on the whole subject of the province
of Pennsylvania; and as for the opposition of the
Quaker population to a defensive war, it was
shown that in no instance had they permitted their
religious principles to obstruct measures for the
protection of the province. It proved, also, that
the Assembly had voted more than a half million
of dollars already, since the war began, besides
being at the expense of erecting forts, raising and
equipping soldiers, fitting out a ship-of-war for
cruising off the coast, and setting on foot a successful expedition against the Indians; and laid
down the proposition that the Proprietaries alone
stood in the way of the harmony of the government and the happiness of the people.

But no impression was yet made by Franklin.
To expedite his business according to the proper
forms, he must first go before the Board of Trade
with his case, who would in turn report their

opinion to the Privy Council. If he could not succeed here, he meant to present the matter directly to Parliament. European politics were so mixed at this time, that colonial affairs went begging for attention. He saw how much longer he was likely to be kept from home than he had expected, and wrote to his wife, January 21st, 1758,—"I begin to think I shall hardly return before this time twelve months. I am for doing effectually what I came about; and I find it requires both time and patience." He found much solace, in his perplexing delays, in the society and conversation of cultivated men; but, after all, he writes that, "at this time of life, domestic comforts afford the most solid satisfaction, and my uneasiness at being absent from my family, and longing desire to be with them, make me often sigh in the midst of cheerful company."

He relaxed no effort to push the business along; there were the lawyers on his own side to supply with the facts of the case, and smaller items to be kept constantly in mind. For a whole year, however, nothing seemed to have been done. That first summer was given up to travelling over England. He was at the Commencement at Cambridge by invitation, where he was received with

marked attention by the heads of the University.
He hunted out the town where his father was
born, and excavated all the traditions possible to
be had respecting his ancestors; consulting the
oldest inhabitants, parish registers, and old tomb-
stones. He found the daughter of his father's
eldest brother, a lady advanced in years. His
father's native town was Ecton; and there had *his*
father, grandfather, and great-grandfather lived
before him. The old home place was a decayed
stone building, but known even then as the
"Franklin House."

The wife of the parish rector told him a great
deal about his family, and carried him out into
the graveyard and pointed out several of the grave-
stones, which were so covered with moss that she
ordered the man to scrub it off with a hard brush
and a basin of water.

Going to Birmingham, he found several of his
wife's relations. When he returned to London
from his tour, his passion for hunting genealogies
as strong as before, he wrote that he had "found
out a daughter of his father's only sister, very old
and never married; a good, clever woman, but
poor; though vastly contented with her situation,
and very cheerful." All his relatives were in

humble life, and some of them very poor; it was his pleasure to hunt them up, claim relationship, and do something to make them remember him.

The papers had been busy, in his absence, swelling the current of popular prejudice against his cause; and he was advised to use their columns in its defence. Accordingly, early in the following year (1759), he came out with a carefully prepared work, entitled the "Historical Review of Pennsylvania." It was not published with his name, yet he received all the abuse it called forth. It was written with great ability and clearness, and was a complete defence of the Assembly and people of Pennsylvania against the assumptions of the Proprietaries. In giving the story of the politics of the province, he reflected with much severity upon the public conduct both of William Penn and his descendants. Through all the attacks which were made on him as the author of the work, he never denied that he did write it, leaving others to infer what they chose. He afterwards denied it, however, in a letter to David Hume, but in such a way as to leave no doubt that it was all compiled and written by his personal direction.

The ministry had been changed just before his

arrival in England, Mr. Pitt being made Prime
Minister. Franklin persistently sought an introduction to this remarkable man, but in vain. He
afterwards said, in alluding to this difficulty, that
Mr. Pitt "was then too great a man, or too much
occupied in affairs of greater moment." Franklin
interested himself deeply in the politics of the
time, and was just the man to advise the ministry
wisely about American affairs. Indeed, it was
by his advice that the conquest of Canada was
adopted as a ministerial measure, and successfully
carried out. Though he could not get the ear of
Pitt, yet his suggestions made Pitt's ministry a
powerful and brilliant one; for, in obedience to
them Wolfe won his famous victory at Quebec,
immortalizing his own name and perpetuating the
power of his country.

In after years, when Pitt was the "great Com-
moner," and stood up in Parliament in eloquent
defence of the liberties of the colonies, he *sought*
Franklin's acquaintance, relying upon him for
much of that information which gave his speeches
such weight and so much of their power.

Little was done for Pennsylvania during 1759.
A new Governor was sent out by the Proprietaries,
—Mr. Hamilton, who had held the office before.

They gave him their explicit instructions, from which he vainly tried, before leaving, to make them deviate.

That summer he went to Scotland, taking his son with him. Distinguished men in that country met him with great respect and cordiality, and among them occur such names as those of Lord Kames, David Hume, and Dr. Robertson. He had been honored with the title of LL. D., some time before, by the University of St. Andrews. He wrote afterwards to Lord Kames, alluding to this visit and the pleasure it gave him:—"On the whole, I must say, I think the time we spent there was six weeks of the *densest* happiness I have met with in any part of my life." So strongly was he attracted to Scotland, he declared that, but for his connections elsewhere, it would be just the country he would like of all others to live in. The "freedom of the city" was presented him while in Edinburgh, "as a mark"—to quote from the record—"of the affectionate respect which the Magistrates and Council have for a gentleman, whose amiable character, greatly distinguished for usefulness to the society which he belongs to, and love to all mankind, had long ago reached them across the Atlantic Ocean."

It consumed three years to finish the business on which he had come to England,—till June, 1760; but it was finally settled to the perfect satisfaction of Franklin and the Assembly, and to the great disappointment of the grasping Proprietaries. The famous Lord Mansfield assisted in drawing up the report of the Board of Trade, which approved of the act of the Pennsylvania Assembly.

The war with France was now coming to an end, and terms of peace were generally talked of among the public men. In the progress of the war, which was but a struggle between the two powers for the control of the American continent, —England had wrested from France Canada, Guadaloupe, and other parts of the West and East Indies, and Africa; the question was, what and how much it would be sound policy to think of holding. Some were for retaining Canada, and some for keeping Guadaloupe. Knowing at least as much as any of them about the controversy, Franklin did not hesitate to take a part in it himself, and to measure opinions and reasonings with such writers as Burke and the Earl of Bath.

He put forth a tract, though without his name, entitled "The Interest of Great Britain Considered;" and argued strongly for the retention of Canada. He had urged its conquest before, and rejoiced when it had fallen into the hands of British power. His views on this subject were those of a statesman; for, said he, "if we keep it (Canada), all the country from the St. Lawrence to the Mississippi will in another century be filled with British people."

The pamphlet produced a marked impression, not less upon the public mind than upon the ministry. Canada, at any rate, was kept fast.

During the summer of 1760, according to his custom while he lived in England, he travelled through the northern part of England, intending to extend his tour to Scotland and Ireland; but he returned through Cheshire and Wales to Bristol and Bath. He found, on his return, that the Pennsylvania Assembly had placed in his hands the money which Parliament had paid back to that province and Delaware, for their outlays during the war,—a sum amounting to some thirty thousand pounds for the first year; this he was requested to invest in the public stocks, and otherwise. By his management of this responsible business he gave the utmost satisfaction to his constituents. The Governor and Proprietaries both labored to prevent his being appointed to do this work, but the Assembly persisted, maintaining its confidence in him throughout.

The next summer (1761), he passed over to the continent; and then began a new epoch in his public life. He visited all the chief cities and towns of Holland and Flanders, and stored his mind with hints that would be of use to him in the future. His studies were naturally interrupted by these changes; yet he was always eager to perform philosophical experiments whenever he could do so. One of his experiments, at this time, was upon the very peculiar properties said to exist in a stone called tourmalin; and another was to prove the theory, then just started, that cold could be produced by evaporation. His experiments in relation to the latter were of remarkable interest. He showed, from them, how it was possible for a man to freeze to death in a hot day of summer. On the principle of evaporation, too, he explained why one's body is never heated above ninety degrees, let the heat around him be as great as it may. He paid a visit to the salt mines of England, on his return to that country, and threw out many interesting and original suggestions on the cause of the salt in the sea; it was his own opinion, and contrary to the general one, that all the water on the globe was salt at first, and that the fresh water to be found in the springs and rivers was the result of distillation. As for the rock salt found in mines, instead of imparting its own qualities to the sea he thought it was itself drawn from the sea, and therefore that the sea is fresher to-day than at the beginning.

He had always been fond of music, from his youth up, and he pursued it as a science as well as an accomplishment. He furnished critical remarks on the old Scotch songs, which were much commended by some of the first men of Scotland as being extremely acute. He also offered some views on the defects of modern music, supporting them with criticisms on one of the compositions of Handel.

When in London, he first saw the famous musical glasses,— a set of tumblers which gave forth music by rubbing the wet fingers around their rims. The invention was but a rude one then, at best; it was necessary first to arrange the glasses on the table, and to tune them by pouring in water until the right note was obtained for each one of them. Franklin thought he could improve on this contrivance, and made the attempt. He

21*

succeeded in making a compact instrument where were several parts and pieces before, and in enlarging the compass of the notes. When complete, he named it the Armonica.

It was a hemisphere in shape, with a socket to fix it on a spindle. The glasses were then arranged on this spindle according to their size, the tones corresponding to the size of the glasses. Then the spindle was fixed in a case horizontally, and turned by a wheel. The person performing on it applied his wet finger to the glasses as they turned round. This novel instrument became very popular in its day, and one lady went to the principal cities of Europe performing on it in public, accompanying it with her voice.

Early in the year 1762, Franklin—now formally recognized as DR. Franklin,—made ready to return home. He was strongly urged to remain in London permanently, and send for his family to come over; and a friend even wrote a letter to Mrs. Franklin, in Philadelphia, laboring to obtain her consent. But she resisted, like her husband. His services were already spoken for by another people, soon to become a nation by themselves. There is no doubt that he would have bettered himself pecuniarily by complying with the request;

but he was already looking in another direction
for the great work of his life.

Edinburgh and Oxford Universities both complimented him with the title of Doctor of Laws,
before leaving. Mr. Hume expressed his sincere
regret at the thought of losing him out of England. Said he—"America has sent us many good
things, gold, silver, sugar, tobacco, indigo, &c. ;
but you are the *first philosopher*, and indeed the
first great man of letters, for whom we are be-
holden to her."

He was jealously watched in all his movements
by the Proprietaries, while in England ; but they
acknowledged that they found no cause of complaint in his conduct, from beginning to end. He
was scrupulous in performing the duties for which
he had been sent over, yet he gave no occasion
for dissatisfaction in his private conduct.

In the latter part of August he set sail to return,
having been absent from home a little more than
five years. He addressed a letter to his friend
Lord Kames, of Scotland, on the eve of going on
shipboard, declaring that he could not leave that
happy island and his many friends in it without
extreme regret, though he was about going to a

country and a people that he loved. In his own words, he fancied he felt "like those who are leaving this world for the next; grief at the parting; fear of the passage; hope of the future." He reached his home in Philadelphia on the first of November.

CHAPTER XI.

FOREIGN AGENT OF THE COLONIES.

HE received, on his return home, the thanks of the Pennsylvania Assembly, and the warm congratulations of his friends. He had been elected to the Assembly every year during his absence, and took his seat immediately on his return. The public thanks were voted to him for his eminent services to America, as well as to Pennsylvania.

His private affairs needed his attention sadly. As Postmaster-General for the colonies still, he travelled for five months of 1763, as far as New Hampshire to the east, making a journey of some sixteen hundred miles, north and south. His daughter travelled with him, he driving for himself in a light carriage. They likewise took a saddle horse along with them, which his daughter rode from Rhode Island to Philadelphia. He was cordially greeted by his old friends in New York, Rhode Island, and Boston.

His health was none too good at this time, which compelled him to favor himself on his journey as much as possible. The people with whom he stopped, too, urged him to eat and drink a great deal more than he wanted, which led him to write his sister in Boston, after reaching home again,—"I am (at home) allowed to know when I have eat and drank enough, am warm enough, and to sit in a place that I like." He recovered his health in due time, and went into active life again.

The western tribes of Indians soon banded together and began to commit barbarities upon the people of the frontier settlements, especially of the Middle States. Troops were raised to repel and punish them without delay. The Assembly of Pennsylvania voted money and appointed commissioners to spend it for war purposes; and Franklin was one of the commissioners. A horrible massacre of inoffensive and friendly Indians occurred, and a regiment of men was raised to go out from Philadelphia and repel the further advances of the rioters. Franklin was one of three or four to address them on behalf of the Assembly. The object of the interview was gained, but none of the bloody murderers of the Indians were ever brought to punishment.

John Penn was sent over as new Governor, in October, 1763. He addressed the Assembly with fair words, which for a time promised harmony between them; but upon that body's framing a militia law, at his own recommendation, which reserved to the several companies of a regiment the power to choose their own officers, subject afterwards to the Governor's selection from *their* choice, ill feelings sprang up again, and disputes of a larger sort soon followed. The subject of a land-tax came up; and the Governor quarrelled with the Assembly on that. The object of this tax was as a basis, or security, for emitting bills of credit, with which to pay the expenses of the war with the Indians. The borders were even then threatened by the savages, and rather than give up safety itself the Assembly yielded to the Governor. But a more bitter feeling toward him than before was the consequence.

They resolved to petition the king, without any further delay, that he would take the government of the province out of the hands of the Proprietaries into his own. Dr. Franklin came forward with one of his effective pamphlets — "Cool

Thoughts on the Present Situation of Public Affairs." He probed the matter to the bottom, and showed the necessity of changing the entire government, so that the proprietary power in it should cease. After a vacation of seven weeks, the Assembly met again (May 14th). Petitions to the king for an immediate change of government came in from all quarters, signed by more than three thousand names. The House took a vote, and resolved to sustain the cause of the petitions. Dr. Franklin drew up still another petition to the king, on behalf of the House.

The subject was debated, pro and con, with much feeling and spirit. The Speaker, Mr. Norris, resigned his seat rather than put his official signature to the petition, and the House at once elected Dr. Franklin to his place. He, of course, signed it without delay. The famous John Dickinson made an eloquent speech against the petition, which was published, with a severely personal preface. Another member, Galloway, published his speech on the other side, to which a preface full of humor and sarcasm was contributed by Dr. Franklin. After a great deal of warm argument, the petitions were sent over to the provincial agent in London, with instructions how to proceed.

But just at that critical time happened to come up in the Assembly the new and startling proposal of the British Ministry to raise money for defraying the expenses of the late war, by imposing stamp duties on the colonies. The news caused great excitement all over the country. At once the Pennsylvania Assembly protested against the measure through their London agent. Dr. Franklin, as Speaker, signed this protest as the last act of his speakership.

A new election came off for members of Assembly in the fall, and by the combination of all the interests on the other side Dr. Franklin was defeated. The men who thought to have their revenge on him in this way found that it would have been more for their interest to have turned in and elected, instead of defeating, him; for being out of public office now, for the first time in fourteen years, the Assembly surprised his enemies by appointing him a special agent to the Court of Great Britain, to take charge of the petition for a change of government, and to look after the general interests of the province. The chagrin of the men who had combined to defeat him in a popular election exceeded all description; it took the form of downright rage.

22

There was no money in the treasury to defray the expenses of a special agent, and it was voted to provide for them in the next money bill that should be passed by the Assembly. A few merchants came forward, in this emergency, and in two hours raised eleven hundred pounds, which they freely loaned to the public for this purpose. Franklin left home for Europe twelve days after he received the new appointment, on the 7th of November, 1764, escorted to Chester, below Philadelphia, by a cavalcade of three hundred citizens. At Chester he was to go on board vessel. The kind feeling shown him on his departure overcame him: he prayed that Heaven would bless his dear friends and "all Pennsylvania." The vessel being hindered a little, he took occasion to write back a letter of advice to his daughter, suggesting that she should not give his political enemies, in his absence, any cause to interpret her own conduct to his prejudice, and to be very circumspect at all times. And he added—"Go to church constantly, whoever preaches. The act of devotion in the Common Prayer Book is your principal business there, and, if properly attended to, will do more towards amending the heart than sermons generally can do." Yet he would not have her despise the sermons, even when she disliked those who preached them; "for the discourse," said he, "is often much better than the man, as sweet and clear waters come through very dirty earth."

He went on shore at Portsmouth after a voyage of thirty days, whence he pushed on to London without delay, and took lodgings as before at Mrs. Stevenson's. When they heard in Philadelphia of his safe arrival out, they rang the bells for joy.

His first duty, as special agent, was to oppose the passage of the Stamp Act by Parliament. The father of the scheme was George Grenville, and with his name it will always be associated. The colonists denied that Parliament had any right to tax them, since they were not represented in that body; and it was a principle of the British Constitution that no man should be taxed save by himself or his representatives. The same principle was recognized in the charters which were given to the colonies. It was argued, on our side, that Parliament could not violate it; but the Ministry had gone too far to turn back now, and so the Stamp Act was passed, though protested against by the colonies and opposed by their agents in London.

Writing home on the event to Charles Thomson,

Franklin said—"Depend upon it, my good neighbor, I took every step in my power to prevent the passing of the Stamp Act. Nobody could be more concerned and interested than myself to oppose it sincerely and heartily. But the tide was too strong against us. The nation was provoked by American claims of independence, and all parties joined by resolving in this act to settle the point. We might as well have hindered the sun's setting. That we could not do. But since it is done, my friend, and it may be long before it rises again, let us make as good a night of it as we can. We may still light candles. Frugality and industry will go a great way towards indemnifying us. Idleness and pride tax with a heavier hand than kings and Parliaments. If we can get rid of the former, we may easily get rid of the latter."

The passage of the Stamp Act produced great excitement in America, and the colonies at once instructed their agents in England to labor for its repeal. The men who had been appointed to distribute the stamps were treated with all sorts of indignities, and finally compelled to resign their posts. None of the stamped paper sent over was permitted to be landed, but was finally sent back again. Early the next year, 1766, such was the opposition to the measure in America, the subject came up before Parliament again. Grenville had been displaced, in the meantime, by the Marquis of Rockingham. It was proposed to repeal the act, in obedience to the piles of petitions from the colonies. The proposal drew out a warm discussion, during which Dr. Franklin was summoned before the bar of the House, to acquaint that body with the real state of things in America.

Both sides put him questions freely, and he answered impromptu. He did not know beforehand what questions they were going to ask him, and he could not therefore prepare his answers; but those answers could not have been more happy and effective. The impression he made on the mind of the House was remarkable. They could not fail to admire his perfect self-possession, his thorough knowledge of the matter inquired about, his dignity, and the propriety of his phrases. The members knew not whether to be lost in admiration or astonishment. It was a remarkable scene, and has always been recalled as perhaps the most memorable in Dr. Franklin's eventful life. They asked him if the Americans would pay the stamp duty if it were to be modified somewhat: "No, never," said he, "unless compelled by force of

22*

arms." He was asked how they would receive
another tax: "Just as they do this," was his answer,—"they will never pay it." He told the
House, in reply to other questions, that his countrymen would never buy British manufactured
goods again, unless this act was repealed; that
they would *never* grow tired of non-importation;
that he knew them as well as any one, and they
had materials enough for their wants, and the industry to work them up; they could and would
make their own clothes; it was once their pride
to indulge in the fashions and manufactures of
Great Britain, but it was their glory now to "wear
their old clothes over again till they can make
new ones."

The stamp act was repealed, after a long and
furious debate; but the sting was left behind, in
what is known as the Declaratory Act, which
affirmed that "Parliament had a right to bind the
colonies in all cases whatsoever." This operated
to cloud the satisfaction which the repeal of the
stamp act had given the colonies. Yet they made
the most of their victory, and to Franklin's personal influence and endeavors was it chiefly due.
They could have sent to England on their business

no man, who would have done for them what he did.

He went over to Germany in the summer of 1766, and paid a visit to Göttingen, among other places. The Universities took up much of his attention. On his return to London, he bent his energies again to the work for which he had come over,—a change of government for Pennsylvania; but, although he succeeded in engaging the serious attention of the ministry in his plan, nothing was actually done in consequence chiefly of the unsettled condition of affairs in the colonies. When the Revolution came, this and other important questions finally settled themselves.

The nature of the relation of the colonies to the mother country next engrossed his attention, and he began to write upon it to his friends in England and at home. What he wrote here had great weight with minds already engaged in discussing the same topic. He agreed that the union might be made a perfect one, if the colonies were allowed to send representatives to Parliament; but it belonged now to Parliament to propose it. "The time has been," said he, "when the colonies might have been pleased with it; they are now indifferent about it; and, if it is much longer delayed, they too will *refuse* it."

There was a season of quiet for him after the repeal of the stamp act, and he improved it for travel. He went to Paris in the autumn of **1767**, in company with his friend Sir John Pringle, and took letters of introduction from the French Ambassador in London to many eminent persons, who received him with cordial respect and esteem. He was presented to the King and the Royal Family. Men of science greeted him warmly. His discoveries in electricity had made him known to them several years before, where they were more truly appreciated than in any other portion of Europe. He little thought, as did any one else, that this first visit to Paris was to prepare the way for his second appearance at the great capital, where he was to perform those distinguished services for a nation which would treasure his name to the latest generation.

Mr. Townshend, Chancellor of the Exchequer, had set in force a revenue act in the interval, which had given great cause of offence to the inhabitants of Massachusetts more particularly. When he got back to London from Paris, news came of popular disturbances in Boston. They disliked the appointment of customs commissioners, and the making of the salaries of their provincial officers dependent on the Crown instead of, as before, on the Assembly of the province. The people of Boston had come together in town meeting, and voted resolves of high spirit. They likewise drew up a paper, and passed it around among the inhabitants, pledging themselves each to the other to do all they could to promote industry and home manufactures, and, after a certain time, not to buy such articles as were named in the paper and imported from abroad. The friends of the ministry looked on these doings as little less than rebellion; while the friends of the colonies themselves could find no ground on which to defend them. Dr. Franklin stepped in with another of his timely publications to allay the excitement, entitled "Causes of the American Discontents before 1768." This he handed to the editor of the London *Chronicle* to publish in that paper; but the editor took the edge all off before it appeared, which led Franklin to say that the man had "drawn the teeth and pared the nails" of his article, so that it could "neither scratch nor bite." Yet it was a judicious and happy effort of the American agent, and did much good in showing

that the discontents in Boston were only the
natural result of the treatment of the colonies for
a long course of years.

The ministry again changed in 1768, Lord Hillsborough becoming Secretary of State for America,
—an office created especially for the care of the
colonies. His control over American affairs was
almost entire. He was upright and honest, but
opinionated and obstinate. He treated Franklin
with much civility at first, holding frequent conversations with him on American affairs; but even
then Franklin foretold a breach between the two
countries. A story was started in England, at the
time, and repeated by his political enemies in
Pennsylvania, that Franklin was in quest of an
office under the ministry, for which he was even
willing to sell the confidence his countrymen had
reposed in him; but his letters about that time
are sufficient to stamp such rumors with the mark
of falsehood. His friends talked of his being
made Governor of Pennsylvania, in case their
form of government was changed; while some of
the most influential inhabitants of Massachusetts
province expressed a desire that he should succeed
Sir Francis Bernard as their Governor, who had

done little but give them trouble from the beginning.

He was about to return home again, his own affairs requiring his attention; and he felt persuaded that his presence was of no service, since he could do nothing which the regular agent could not as well do without him. Just then he received the appointment of agent for the colony of Georgia; and he deemed it best to wait for the arrival of his instructions. This delayed him until other matters crowded in to prolong his stay much beyond all his calculations. It was in the fall of that year that he was invited to dine, with fifteen other gentlemen, with the King of Denmark who was then in London.

He never lost his interest in his philosophical inquiries and studies, and, among other suggestions, he wrote home to urge the colonists to plant mulberry trees and raise silkworms, as a profitable branch of domestic industry. This, perhaps, was as much from his desire that his countrymen should produce their own clothing as from any other; for he repeatedly addressed them in favor of holding out against the importation or use of British commodities. As the petitions of the colonists produced no effect with Parliament or the ministry, he advised them to prepare to support themselves.

Late in the year, he received the agency of the New Jersey colony also, of which his son was the Governor. The boundary between East and West Jersey was left to his care, with other matters. He had occasion, just at that time, to express his views upon the probability of the colonies becoming quiet again; but from the first he solemnly declared that nothing would satisfy and pacify the people of America but a clear repeal of all the laws designed to collect a revenue from them without their consent.

Parliament took the matter up with all seriousness, in the month of April, 1770. The ministry were persuaded of the determination of the colonies, after three years' holding out, to withhold their trade as long as the new revenue laws were on the books, and they concluded to wipe them all out, abolishing taxes of every sort for the Americans except a tax on tea. It was in no sense, however, a movement for redressing the wrongs of which the colonists complained; but a stroke of commercial policy alone. The duty on the single article of tea, too, was calculated to let the people of this country feel that Parliament was still supreme.

The effect was to exasperate and arouse the colonists more than ever. Dr. Franklin was in continual correspondence with the home governments, and with his friends, and some of his letters were secretly obtained and sent back to England to the ministers. It was thrown out that he would lose his office as Postmaster-General, in return for what he had written home about the ministry. The papers abused and traduced him, probably hoping to force him to resign; but that he would not do: he thought that as he had, by close attention and unwearied industry, made the post-office revenues worth what they were, he would fix upon the ministry the odium of turning him out of office, and not relieve them voluntarily of such a load himself.

As these letters made a great deal of talk in their day, it would be as well to know what he had to say about their authorship. "It was true," said he, "I did write them, and they were written in compliance with another duty, that to my country; a duty quite distinct from that of Postmaster." He said that he had behaved in this matter just as he did a few years before on a similar oc-

23

casion, when the ministry were "ready to *hug*" him for the help he rendered them. Even if they did remove him from office, he would not therefore change his political opinions. He did not hold that, because he held an office under the ministry, he was obliged to act *with* the ministry in all matters. His rule was, "never to turn aside in public affairs through views of private interest; but to go straight forward in doing what appears to me right at the time, leaving the consequences with Providence."

Massachusetts likewise appointed him her agent, at this stage of affairs, well knowing his sentiments through the letters which were written by him to some of the leading men of the province. This appointment nettled Lord Hillsborough more than all. The ministry had had more trouble, thus far, with Massachusetts than with any other colony; and to find Franklin, after having presented the protests of several of the other colonies, accredited as the agent of Massachusetts likewise, was a little too much for their temper. Lord Hillsborough broke out in a fit of anger, when Franklin went to present his credentials, and the scene became an interesting one, to say the least. He denied the fact of Franklin's appointment as agent at all.

Franklin answered him, coolly and calmly, that his letters had been brought by the last ships. Hillsborough denied that such an agency could be entrusted to any man without the assent and co-operation of the Governor; on this point, Franklin took issue, showing that the Colonial Assemblies always had appointed such agents as they chose, and without asking the consent or caring for the opposition of any royal Governor whatever.

He finally handed Hillsborough the proof of his appointment, in the form of the vote of the House appointing him, saying to him as he did so —"Will your Lordship please to look at it?" He took the paper, but did not deign to open it; breaking out into angry declamation, he denounced the whole system of appointing agents, and said that he would have nothing to do with one of them unless they were regularly appointed and their appointment approved by the Governor. And after more talk of the same sort, and expostulations by Franklin, he handed back the latter his papers without any further examination of them. It was very rude of his Lordship; but it incited Franklin to tell him, as he was leaving his presence, that it was of little consequence whether the appointment was recognized by him or not,

for he was persuaded no agent whatever could be
of any use there to the colonies.

Dr. Franklin was at this time the special agent
in London of four colonies, and he was closely engaged with their affairs. In the following year,
1771, he found leisure for another tour, which he
made in England. He found this annual recreation necessary for the preservation of his health,
which was beginning to suffer somewhat from his
excessive confinement to business when in London. He went, this year, to Leeds, to Manchester,
and to Litchfield, at each of which places he met
distinguished men, whom he assisted about their
philosophical experiments, and with whom he was
in correspondence on scientific studies for years
afterward. During this summer tour, he went
into Wales, Scotland, and Ireland; he had not
been in the last named country before. All parties offered him most respectful welcome. At
Dublin he met Lord Hillsborough, and dined with
him at the Lord Lieutenant's. Hillsborough
pressed him to stop at his house on his northward
journey, which he could not well refuse. He spent
four days there, and was treated with surprising
civility, after the recent scene which had occurred
between them. He took the distinguished Ameri-

can agent out to ride over the country in his phaeton, and even threw his own overcoat over his shoulders, lest he should take cold from exposure. Franklin was at a loss how to explain it.

The Irish Parliament received him with honor, inviting him to a seat within the bar. In Scotland he renewed his old friendships, staying with Lord Kames and David Hume. He felt more strongly attached to Scotland and its people than ever. He employed his influence to procure from Edinburgh University honorary degrees for Dr. Cooper, President Stiles, and Professor Winthrop, of Harvard College.

He met his son-in-law, Richard Bache, on his return to England, never having seen him before, though he had been the husband of his daughter for four years; and he wrote home that he was much pleased with him and his connections. He also paid a visit to Dr. Shipley, Bishop of Asaph, for whom he had conceived a very warm friendship, and whom he used to call the "good Bishop." At his house, he began the composition of his autobiography, which he never finished. His country seat was in Hampshire, and his family-circle exceedingly attractive. Franklin continued

23*

to correspond with the Bishop and one of his daughters as long as they both lived.

Even then he seriously thought of going home again to Pennsylvania; he was grown tired and disgusted with the delays of his business, and become quite willing to leave a position full of annoyance and productive of no sort of public good. He was in his sixty-seventh year now, and wrote home to his son that he grew homesick; he was also afraid of the infirmities of age coming suddenly upon him, so as to prevent his returning home altogether. "I have also," said he, "some important affairs to settle before my death, a period I ought now to think cannot be far distant." He loved his friends in England very strongly, and could have contented himself to live and die with them, but that he also loved so well the country from which he had been so long an exile.

CHAPTER XII.

STEPS TO THE REVOLUTION.

LORD HILLSBOROUGH did not treat Franklin very handsomely, after his return to London, notwithstanding his cordial manner at his country home; he refused to see him several times, and his servant once used insulting language before the door, while Franklin sat waiting in the carriage. He never called on his lordship again, but, as he expressed it, "we have only abused one another at a distance."

A popular controversy sprung up on the relative value of *pointed* and *blunt* conductors, about this time, in which Dr. Franklin necessarily took a part. He showed the public, by a series of experiments, that pointed were far safer than the blunt, because they insensibly draw the electricity from the clouds, while the latter cannot always carry off the entire amount of the fluid presenting itself, which, therefore leads to an explosion. In the height of the discussion, the king changed the pointed conductors on the queen's palace for blunt ones; but Franklin thought that settled nothing, either way. So far as he was himself concerned, he could have wished that he would reject them altogether, as of no use; "for," added he, "it is only since he thought himself and family safe from the thunder of Heaven, that he dared to use his own thunder in destroying his innocent subjects." To make fun of the whole matter, the following epigram, among other things, was published: —

> "While you, great GEORGE, for safety hunt,
> And sharp conductors change for blunt,
> The Empire's out of joint;
> Franklin a wiser course pursues,
> And all your thunder fearless views,
> By keeping to the *point.*"

The story of the various steps that led to the final outbreak between the inhabitants of the colonies and the mother country is too long to be inserted in a biography of this kind; it is enough merely to sketch the part which Franklin took in the various proceedings which finally culminated in revolt and revolution.

Lord Hillsborough was removed from the charge of the American Department, and Lord Dartmouth appointed in his place. Franklin handed Lord Dartmouth, at their first interview, a petition from the Massachusetts Assembly to the king. It was respecting their Governor's (Hutchinson) receiving his salary from the Crown instead of from the people, as heretofore; a practice against all former custom, and bringing into contempt the ancient prerogative of the Assembly. Lord Dartmouth advised that it should not be presented to the king just then, on account of former irritation. Dr. Franklin showed him why he thought the present was as fit as any other time for the purpose, but concluded at last not to press the matter, but to send home an account of the conversation held between them upon it.

Next came news to the people of Massachusetts that the salaries of the Judges, as well as that of the Governor, had been made dependent on the Crown. The inhabitants of Boston at once held a town meeting, and drew up a strong protest, asserting that it was but another link in the chain which was forging for their bondage. They voted that copies of the bold and energetic resolutions which were passed by them should be sent to all

the other towns in the province, with an invitation
to them to hold similar meetings, and express
their sentiments with equal freedom. The Massachusetts Governor was greatly incensed at these
proceedings of the people, and, in his letters to
England, laid the whole blame on Franklin. He
openly charged to the Ministry that these claims
of the colonies "were prepared in England in a
more full manner than ever before, with a manifest
design and tendency to revive a flame which was
near expiring." He also charged that it was the
design to make a stand for these claims in Massachusetts first, and afterwards in the other colonies.
Franklin was called by him "the great director in
England" of the whole plan.

It is sufficient, however, to offer a general denial
to all such charges. While Hutchinson was making
them, the friends of Franklin were complaining
of his being lukewarm in their interest. Still, he
held fast to all his old opinions on the relations of
the two countries, and advised the colonies not to
consent to part with a single right that belonged
to them. But he probably did not suit all the
enthusiastic ones, by reason of his wise moderation ; he always proposed to them to make haste

slowly, knowing that events must work with them instead of against them.

He republished the doings of the people of Boston, as soon as they reached him in London, and wrote a preface for the pamphlet. The temper of his own production made friends and hearers for the rest of the publication. Pretty soon after, the Massachusetts Assembly met and passed similar resolutions, which they forwarded to Dr. Franklin to present to the king. He repaired to Lord Dartmouth as soon as he received them, and told him the case would admit of no more delay; his Lordship promised to deliver the petition, therefore, to his Majesty.

Dr. Franklin not only wrote and published, at this time, the preface to the doings of the inhabitants of Boston, already spoken of, but likewise a couple more articles, to which, however, he did not put his name; they caused wide remark, and are known by the titles of " Rules for Reducing a Great Empire to a Small One," and " An Edict by the King of Prussia." They were full of dry humor, which produced more effect than could have been secured by any other style of composition. In the summer of 1773, while absent in the country again, he beguiled his time with abridging the Book of Common Prayer, of which a handsome edition was printed, though it never came into use.

In the latter part of the year 1772, he had procured and sent to Massachusetts certain letters which were written by Governor Hutchinson and Lieutenant-Governor Oliver of that province to a certain member of Parliament. They were private letters, but they dealt with public affairs in the colonies. They represented that all the troubles on this side were fomented by a few restless and intriguing spirits, but that they could be put an end to by employing a military force that should overawe these leaders. Franklin sent over these very important letters from motives of the purest patriotism, believing that his countrymen should know what was said. He said himself of the letters, when he forwarded them—"I am not at liberty to tell through what channel I received it (the correspondence); and I have engaged that it should not be printed, nor copies taken of the whole or any part of it; but I am allowed to let it be seen by some men of worth in the province, for their satisfaction only."

Franklin was greatly vilified and abused in England for having forwarded these letters to

America. But they produced the effect that was intended. They were handed round among the first men of Massachusetts, and Mr. John Adams, afterwards President, but then a country lawyer, carried them in his pocket while travelling a court circuit. The provincial Assembly passed a vote of condemnation upon the letters, averring that they were calculated only to make mischief and sow the seeds of discord. They also voted to petition the king for the instant removal of both Hutchinson and Oliver. Franklin received this petition on its arrival; and as Lord Dartmouth was absent at the time in the country, he sent it to him. It was soon presented to the king. Governor Hutchinson's letters having meantime been published in Boston, they found their way in type very soon to London. The discovery of their loss from the papers of the gentleman to whom they were originally addressed excited suspicion against a certain other gentleman who alone was known to have been permitted access to them, and a duel grew out of it.

At this juncture, Dr. Franklin thought it necessary to come forward with his own statement. He publicly took upon himself the responsibility of having sent the obnoxious letters to America,

24

which he did merely to screen an innocent gentleman to whom suspicion was wrongly directed;
and the natural consequence was that all tongues
and pens were instantly turned against him. A
chancery suit was instituted against him also, but
was finally abandoned.

Presently he received a summons to appear
before the Privy Council, who were considering
the Massachusetts Assembly petition for the removal of their Governor and Lieutenant-Governor.
The petition was read in his hearing, and then he
was questioned as to what he had to say in its
favor. After some conversation, it appeared that
Hutchinson and Oliver had engaged counsel to
defend them. To this Franklin objected, saying
that he did not understand that counsel was to be
employed against the petition, and that he did not
conceive any point of law involved which required
a lawyer's arguments; he held it, rather, to be "a
question of civil and political jurisprudence,"
which could readily be decided by the facts in
hand. As the Governor and Lieutenant-Governor
had counsel, he desired that the Assembly should
have counsel likewise; to procure which, and
allow time for preparation, the space of three
weeks was granted.

All sorts of stories were bruited about London in relation to the bluff reception Franklin had met with before the Council, and to the way the Solicitor-General, who was the counsel for Hutchinson and Oliver, had treated him. Franklin engaged two distinguished barristers for the Assembly. The result of the hearing was, their Lordships dismissed the petition, characterizing it as "groundless, vexatious, and scandalous, and calculated only for the seditious purpose of keeping up a spirit of clamor and discontent in the provinces." This Report was approved by the king, who thereupon dismissed the petition. Could a more ingenious way have been devised for alienating and exasperating a brave and high-spirited people, who certainly were *as much* entitled to the common birthright of freemen as their own kin who chanced to live in England?

On the very next day, Franklin was officially notified of his removal from the office of Deputy Postmaster-General for the colonies. He had looked for this, yet it made him indignant when the base return finally came. He kept down his feelings, however, resolved to remain in perfect control of his temper, and knowing that when he lost that he would part with his power to be of further service to his countrymen. After this he kept away from the ministry, wishing to have nothing more to do with them. It was his intention to return immediately home; but, as before, circumstances prevented. This was in the autumn of 1774, and he was sixty-eight years of age.

Hearing that the colonies were about to assemble in a Continental Congress, he waited in patience to learn what step would be taken by them next. The arrival of Josiah Quincy, Jr., in England, son of his old friend in Massachusetts, brought him much comfort and consolation; he got the latest advices by him about the feeling of his countrymen. He was just the man to put him in possession of the most secret sentiments and designs of the American leaders. For some four months, he and Dr. Franklin enjoyed one another's society almost daily.

The Doctor was getting ready to leave England as early as possible the next year, with fondest hopes of once more joining the delightful family circle from which he had been separated for ten years, when the sad intelligence of his wife's sudden death reached him. She was stricken with paralysis, and survived the shock but five days. They had been man and wife forty-four years, and

STEPS TO THE REVOLUTION.

their married life had been one of perfect harmony. He wrote of her, many years after her death, to a young lady,—"Frugality is an enriching virtue; a virtue I never could acquire myself; but I was once lucky enough to find it in a wife, who therefore became a fortune to me."

In December of that year (1774), about the middle of the month, he received from America the petition of the first Continental Congress to King George, accompanied with a letter from the President of that new body to all the colonial agents in London, desiring them to present the petition. The other agents, with the exception of two beside Franklin, declined acceding to the request, in consequence of having received no instructions from their several colonies. But these three—Franklin, Bollan, and Lee,—carried the petition to Lord Dartmouth, who kept it in his hands one day, and then engaged to deliver it. He afterwards informed them that it had been received by the king, who would at once lay it before Parliament for consideration. It was done, but no allusion whatever was made to it in the king's speech. The agents asked to be heard in support of it at the bar of the House, but were refused the privilege. It was soon after rejected by a de-

24*

cided vote. In the course of the debate, the colonists were spoken of with contempt, and an armed force was threatened to keep them in subjection.

Franklin saw that a rupture could not long be avoided, if matters went on in this way. He visited Lord Chatham (the elder Pitt) at his country place by invitation, where a free conversation was held on American affairs; his Lordship expressing the highest esteem and the sincerest sympathy for the people of the colonies, and hoping that they would continue firm, and remain united in the defence of their rights. Something passed between them relative to the desire of the colonists for independence; but Franklin assured his Lordship that no such thing had for once been seriously thought of. Yet he knew too well that the treatment which the Ministry were visiting upon the Americans would surely force them to independence at last.

Two of his influential friends, seeing what a critical turn matters were taking, urged him to come forward and make one more effort to bring about a reconciliation; they assured him that the Ministers were not all of one mind, but that some of them really desired a restoration of the old friendship. They asked him to draw up a plan of agreement, such as would be acceptable both to himself and the colonists. He consented after a time to do so, and, at their next meeting, handed them a paper containing the heads of seventeen different articles, styled by him *Hints*, which could readily be thrown into the form of a compact. When they read them, they raised objections to some of the articles, and had their doubts about others; but they made copies, and promised to show them around in ministerial circles, where they enjoyed intimacies.

Franklin had an interview on America, likewise, with Lord Howe, who was very anxious that he should effect a reconciliation if possible. He went to the seat of Lord Chatham, too, who spoke in high praise of the proceedings of Congress, saying that by reason of their calm, wise, and moderate conduct, they formed "the most honorable assembly of statesmen since those of the ancient Greeks and Romans in the most virtuous times." He also passed a night at the residence of Lord Camden, who held similar opinions on American affairs with those of Chatham.

When he got back to London from this little visit, Lord Howe assured him that both Lord

North and Lord Dartmouth were disposed to bring about an accommodation, and asked him his opinion of sending over a Commissioner to America to inquire into the grievances of the colonists, and to agree on some terms of pacification. Franklin said he thought well of it. Lord Howe's sister, who was present, remarked that she wished he was himself going to America as Commissioner, instead of the General to command the armies there. His Lordship had perused the Hints which Franklin had before drawn up as a basis of pacification, and took a copy of them out of his pocket: but he said that the proposal was much too hard to be accepted. He therefore wished that Franklin would make another effort and offer. This the latter promised to do, though he did not believe it would be of any more avail. He did accordingly frame another proposition, based on the petition of Congress to the King, and sent the same to Lord Howe, who communicated it to persons of high standing in the ministerial party.

Hearing from Lord Stanhope that Chatham was going to offer a motion in the House of Lords the next day, and that he desired him to be present, he determined not to miss the opportunity. The

very next day, January 20th, 1775, he received a
message from Lord Chatham himself, asking him
to be there. He was punctual, and met Chatham
as expected. Lord Chatham remarked to him
that his presence at the debate that day would be
of more service to America than his own. Taking
Franklin by the arm, he conducted him by the
passage to the door opening near the throne. A
door-keeper came up and told him that none could
be taken in by that door except the eldest sons or
brothers of peers; upon which his Lordship, who
was lame from gout, limped back with him to the
door near the bar. A knot of gentlemen stood
around, waiting for the peers who were to intro-
duce them to the floor. Chatham handed him
over to the door-keepers, saying in a voice which
all could hear,—" This is Dr. Franklin, whom I
would have admitted into the House." The door
opened with no further delay. Those who saw
Franklin with Lord Chatham, but did not know
of there being any commerce between them, were
rather confounded, and fell to wondering what it
meant. They had not long to wait in order to
find out.

Lord Chatham rose very soon and moved that
the troops be withdrawn from Boston; the motion

was debated with warmth, but finally lost. Lord Chatham told the House that his motion was only introductory to a plan of reconciliation which he had it in mind to bring forward. That plan he did show to Franklin, a week after this debate, and asked him to consider it at his leisure. The latter raised several objections to it; but as it did not altogether satisfy Chatham, either, it was thought best that it should, at any rate, be brought before the House of Lords, if only to open the way for a reconciliation on some other basis.

It was so submitted, on the 1st of February. Dr. Franklin was admitted to the House as before. The audience was large and profoundly interested. Lord Chatham made one of his most noble efforts in behalf of it, and in favor of adopting some just measures for an immediate and permanent reconciliation with the colonies. His speech was so grand, so full of power, so overflowing with his matchless eloquence, it has become historical. But in spite of all he could do, assisted by the powerful talents of such men as Lord Camden, Lord Temple, and others, the bill was lost by a majority of two to one. Lord Sandwich, who assailed it, was especially abusive and passionate. He said he would not believe it proceeded from a peer of the realm, but he rather believed it to be the work of some man from the other side of the Atlantic.   He turned upon Dr. Franklin, who was leaning on the bar at the time, and, looking straight at him, savagely remarked that "he fancied he had in his eye *the person* who drew it up,—one of the bitterest and most mischievous enemies this country had ever known." Lord Chatham instantly took the whole responsibility of it upon himself.   He was the more willing to own its authorship, since several of them professed to think so meanly of it; for if it was so weak, he should be unwilling that any one else should be censured for it.   He further stated, that it had been reckoned his vice heretofore, "not to be apt to take advice; but he made no scruple to declare, that, if he were the first minister of this country, and had the care of settling this momentous business, he should not be ashamed of publicly calling to his assistance a person so perfectly acquainted with the whole of American affairs as the gentleman alluded to and so injuriously reflected on; one, he was pleased to say, whom all Europe held in high estimation for his knowledge and wisdom, and ranked with our Bayles and

Newtons; who was an honor, not to the Englisl nation only, but to human nature !"

His "Hints" were considered and talked about, on this side and that, subsequently to the rejection of Lord Chatham's bill by the House of Lords; but nothing promised to result from it all. There were two or three persons, certainly, among the Ministry, each of whom wanted to be sent to America as a Commissioner to adjust the difficulties; and several plans were tried for the sake of getting Franklin to subscribe to just points enough to warrant their appointment in that capacity; but the American sage kept the rights and interests of his countrymen in mind rather than the personal ambition of certain public men in England. For ten long years he had held steadfastly to the important work on which he was despatched to England; and he displayed an amount of enthusiasm and a persistency of purpose that was truly wonderful, when it is considered that he had been separated from his countrymen so long, and had few or no opportunities to understand exactly how they felt, or how common was the disposition to resist openly. He of course was regularly apprised of what was transpiring in the colonies; but he needed personal

contact with his countrymen to kindle his patriotism to that glow at which it would most effectively
aid him in his purposes. Under the circumstances,
therefore, he did what it seems no other man of
his time could have done for America. He laid
the claims of the colonies on a foundation so
broad and deep that neither the prejudices of
ministers nor the passions of the populace could
shake them.

His work in England had drawn to a close.
There was nothing more for him to do. His
friends were more his friends than ever, and they
sent him back across the ocean with every expression of esteem and attachment. He left word with
two of the other agents that it was barely possible
that he might return on business for Pennsylvania
in the autumn, but not again for Massachusetts.

He set sail from England on the 21st of March,
1775, being now sixty-nine years old; and he arrived at Philadelphia on the 5th of May. The
battles of Lexington and Concord—those opening
scenes of the seven years' drama—were fought
while he was upon the ocean. He beguiled the
long time of his voyage with writing an account
of his efforts while in England to prevent a col-
lision between the mother country and her colo-

25

nies, and to perpetuate their former friendship. And he lost no opportunity, either, to experiment philosophically while on the deep. He discovered that the water in the Gulf stream is warmer than the water on either side of it; a matter which he explained after philosophical methods.

On the very next day after he arrived home, the Pennsylvania Assembly chose him a delegate to the second Continental Congress, which was held in Philadelphia on the 10th of the month. The news of the 19th of April, at Lexington and Concord, had aroused the colonists from one end of the land to the other. Franklin wrote to Dr. Priestly at once, that "the breach between the two countries is grown wider, and in danger of becoming irreparable."

He was with those who were foremost in the Congress to unite now in open resistance to England. He believed that the time for protests and petitions was passed. The Congress did send over another petition, though there was strong opposition to the step; still, all were ready to keep the door open for reconciliation as late and long as possible. Franklin was now an active member of Congress, though in his seventieth year, besides serving as Chairman of the Committee of Safety, appointed by the Pennsylvania Assembly. The latter was a position which required constant labor and care. For eight months he served upon this committee with all the laborious zeal of a young man. He wrote—"My time was never more fully employed; in the morning at six, I am at the Committee of Safety, which committee holds till near nine; when I am at Congress, and that sits till four in the afternoon." Young men, in these days, do not usually work any harder than that.

He was before the general sentiment in the matter of a separate and independent government, and on the 21st of July he presented a plan of a confederacy of the colonies to the Congress. No action was then had upon it, but it formed the groundwork of operations in that direction, about a year later. It amounted, in fact, to a declaration of independence. Congress proceeded to establish a general post office system, the old one being destroyed by the hostile relations of the two countries; and Franklin was made Postmaster-General, with a salary of a thousand dollars a year. He was empowered to make what post-routes and appoint such postmasters under him as he chose. In the raising and organization of the army, which was the first matter before Congress, he performed excellent and timely service. He was placed, too, on a number of important committees, on all of which he served industriously. He was a member of the Secret Committee of Congress, among others; whose duty it was to obtain cannon, muskets, and ammunition, as well as to procure every variety of military supplies and afterward distribute them among the troops and such armed vessels as were in the Continental service. It required great caution and foresight to import these necessary articles of war, and steer clear of subjecting them to the capture of the enemy's vessels which were cruising everywhere.

He likewise turned his hand to a plan for emitting paper currency; but his suggestions were not all adopted by the Congress, which doubtless was the cause of the depreciation of that currency after a short trial. When Washington took command of the American army at Cambridge, Dr. Franklin was sent, with Benjamin Harrison and Thomas Lynch, to the camp, to devise a plan for the greatest possible efficiency of the army. The meeting between these distinguished persons took place at Washington's headquarters on the 18th day of October; and the several colonies of New England were represented. The interview was prolonged through several days; and the result reached proved satisfactory to the committee and to General Washington.

He had been elected a member of the Pennsylvania Assembly in his absence, so that when he returned he found himself obliged to attend daily upon the Assembly, the Congress, and the Committee of Safety for Pennsylvania; but he gave Congress the preference when the hours of meeting interfered. On the 29th of November, Congress appointed a Committee of Secret Correspondence, for the purpose of keeping up regular communication with those who favored America in Europe, whether in England, Scotland, and Ireland, or on the continent. Dr. Franklin was, of course, assigned an important place on this committee. He forthwith laid a train by which the committee could at an early day receive intelligence of what was going on in Europe. He was very industrious with his always serviceable pen in this direction.

A plan was set on foot to induce the people of the Canadas to take part in the Congress; but it soon fell through. The Canadians and the colonists could not be expected to become sudden friends, after past experiences, on no better basis than that of a common hatred of the measures of Great Britain. But Congress sent a commission to Canada, composed of Dr. Franklin, Samuel Chase, and Charles Carroll, to look after the army operations which were going forward in that quarter, and to promise the people of Canada all the help they wanted in setting up a government for themselves.

They left on the 20th of March, 1776, but did not arrive in Montreal until the last of April. The roads were in such condition that they could not travel any faster. And it was a very inopportune time, too, when they did arrive; for the American army, under Montgomery and Arnold, had begun their retreat after the disaster before Quebec, and it was not to be supposed that the Canadians cared to treat with the new commissioners on such a subject, just then, if, indeed, they ever had been ready to treat. Dr. Franklin was exposed to the most inclement weather during the journey, being compelled to sleep out in the woods in some parts of it; and this, for a man of seventy, might be thought rather hard usage. He remained two weeks in Montreal, and then turned his steps homeward again, leaving the other commissioners behind. He reached Albany after much trouble, and went thence in the private carriage of General Schuyler to New York, and finally arrived home in the fore-part of June.

CHAPTER XIII.

MINISTER TO FRANCE.

HE now gave his whole time to his duties as a member of Congress. The subject of independence was broached, and immediately arrested general attention. All things were ripe for the movement. Virginia directed her delegates to propose it in the Congress. Her request was obeyed by the famous Richard Henry Lee. The debate drew out the fact that the greater part of that body was prepared to take the final step towards independence. In that immortal debate, such men as John Dickinson, John Adams, Roger Sherman, Livingston, and Lee participated. A committee was selected to draw up a Declaration of Independence, which consisted of John Adams, Jefferson, Franklin, Sherman, and Livingston. Jefferson drafted the Declaration, but Franklin and Adams made a few verbal alterations. It was debated for three days, and on the 4th of July passed by an emphatic vote. While the members were signing their names to the new Declaration, Hancock, whose bold hand seems to overshadow all the rest, made the remark—"We must be unanimous; there must be no pulling different ways; we must all hang together." "Yes," said Franklin, "we must, indeed, all *hang together*, or most assuredly we shall all hang separately."

In the measures taken immediately after to set an effective government in operation, Dr. Franklin took a profound interest, and his talents were always at the command of the Congress. The important letters, documents, schemes, and discussions with which his name was intimately connected, are more numerous than is popularly thought.

Congress having at length decided to make an attempt to form foreign alliances, the colonies being now an independent power, the first thought was to make approaches to France; the general instinct was, that she would see that such an alliance against England would be for her interests every way. Accordingly, three commissioners were appointed to reside near the Court of France, and attend to the interests of the American colonies. They were Dr. Franklin, Silas Deane, and Arthur Lee. Deane was in France already, engaged in procuring and sending out munitions of war; Lee was in England, where Franklin left him; and Franklin would have but to cross the seas to make the trio complete.

On the 26th of October, 1776, he took his departure from Philadelphia, to perform the crowning public services of his life. His two grandsons went in his company. On the following day they went aboard the ship Reprisal, carrying sixteen guns. He had placed all the money he could raise before leaving home—between three and four thousand pounds—at the disposal of Congress. The vessel was chased by British cruisers, but not overhauled. The captain took two British prizes, however, off the French coast.

Dr. Franklin was set on shore at Auray, whence he went by land to Nantes, a distance of seventy miles. Here he sought rest from the fatigue of his voyage and journey at a country seat near by. Nobody knew beforehand of his coming. Even the fact of his appointment was kept secret by Congress. After eight days he set out for Paris, arriving there on the 21st of December. There was a great deal of talk in all circles in the French capital, when it was known that he had arrived in the country, and all parties puzzled their wits to make out in exactly what capacity he had come. Mr. Deane was already in Paris, and Mr. Lee arrived the next day. Dr. Franklin soon took lodgings at Passy, a pretty little village near Paris, where he continued to make his home for the whole time he was in France.

His antecedent life had prepared the way for his cordial reception. He was long before known as a philosopher, as the author of "Poor Richard," and for his frank but bold conduct in the face of the English ministry, while the American cause still claimed a hearing before Parliament and the King. The people of Paris looked on him as a sage, and paid him the full reverence due such an exalted character. It was said of the effect produced by his coming, that " diplomatic etiquette did not permit him often to hold interviews with the ministers, but he associated with all the distinguished personages who directed public opinion." The people of France took him as a personal representative of his countrymen, and regarded his serene countenance as like their own. He was described as joining " to the demeanor of

Phocion the spirit of Socrates." The old and the young made common court to him, and esteemed it almost a royal privilege to gain admission to his house at Passy. He did not have to put himself to much trouble to negotiate; "his virtues and his renown negotiated for him."

His portraits were to be seen everywhere. His venerable looking head was on medallions of every variety, of sizes suitable to be set in snuff-box lids, or worn in rings. He had worn a huge wig, while in England, agreeably to the fashion of the times; but he put it off, after he went to France, and wore a fur cap on his head in place of it. After a time, he went without this; and in the best portrait which was ever painted of him, that by Duplessis, he shows none but his own hair, sparse on the top of his head, but flowing down freely over his shoulders. He likewise wore spectacles, a little later in life, whenever he went from home.

The business of the Commissioners was to offer a plan to the French Court for a treaty of commerce with the American nation, and to try and obtain, at the cost of the United States, eight line-of-battle ships; also to borrow money, obtain and send forward military supplies, and fit out armed vessels under the new flag of the United States, should the French government offer no objection.

But while France was willing to help the colonies, it was not for her interest just then to break with England. The Commissioners made a great many valuable friends, though but little visible headway in their business. The people of France were much more demonstrative than the ministry. The news of the reverses in America, too, did not have the effect to make very enthusiastic friends for the colonists, at that particular time. Canada was cleared of our troops; the battle of Long Island had been fought and lost to us; the British had compelled us to evacuate New York; and General Howe was in possession of forts Washington and Lee, on the Hudson. Washington was retreating with the ragged remnants of an army through New Jersey, and the people of the country through which he passed were losing their faith in the cause. Congress, too, had fled from Philadelphia to Baltimore. To ask France to step out before the world at such a time and become the open friend of our falling fortunes, much less to become the voluntary champion of

26

our cause, would have been preposterous, if not a token of insanity.

For all that, the Commissioners received secret intimations and pledges of sympathy and support from the Ministry, though they were not permitted to hold audience with the King. It was likewise told them that two millions of livres would come to them soon, through a private hand, to be used on behalf of the United States. The pretence was that the money was the free contribution of a few generous individuals, who entertained a deep sympathy with the American cause, and did not ask that the money should be repaid until after peace was declared. But the truth was, the money came from the royal treasury; and so the Commissioners understood it. And knowing this, and realizing also what was the determination among their countrymen to hold out until independence was achieved, Franklin and his associates felt sure that France would in good time come out and openly side with America.

In the early autumn of 1777, General Burgoyne was captured, with all his army, by the northern army under General Gates; and this put a brighter face on matters at once. The Commissioners improved the fortunate occasion to present the Court with an account of the new state of things, and to urge again their proposal for a treaty. The King and Ministry had been waiting for just such a fortunate change in American affairs, and were ready now to make a favorable response to the American agents. M. Gerard, the Secretary of the King's Council, waited on them, and assured them that, by the advice of his Council, the King had resolved to acknowledge the independence of the United States, and to enter into a treaty of friendship and commerce with them. The King further desired to assure them that he wished to take no sort of advantage of the present condition of the United States, to exact terms which they would not care to comply with in more prosperous times, but that he wished to deal with them on fair and equal terms, being resolved to aid them in their efforts to establish an independent nation by every means at his command. It was to be expected, of course, that war with England would grow out of it; but he exacted no indemnities on that account, only desiring the United States to make a pledge not to surrender *their entire independence* in any treaty of peace which they might make with England, nor ever return to subjection again to British rule.

The new treaty was signed on the 6th day of February, 1788, and a messenger was sent over at once with the tidings to America, where it was received with tokens of universal joy and gratitude. To the address, perseverance, skill, and personal popularity of Dr. Franklin the people of the United States felt that they owed this most desirable result.

The independence of America having thus been proclaimed, of course the Court could no longer decline to give an audience to its agents and commissioners. They made their public appearance at Versailles accordingly. In the accounts which were given of this notable ceremony, Franklin is spoken of as being accompanied by a large number of Americans and foreigners, led by curiosity to witness the scene. "His age," says one, "his venerable aspect, the simplicity of his dress, everything fortunate and remarkable in the life of this American, contributed to excite public attention. The clapping of hands and other expressions of joy indicated that warmth of enthusiasm which the French are more susceptible of than any other people." When he crossed the court to pass to the office of the Minister of Foreign Affairs, the crowd waited for him until he came in sight, when they greeted him with acclamations. Whenever he made his public appearance in Paris, he was the recipient of similar attentions. At so fashionable a Court as that of France, he was made rather more of by reason of his republican dress. Madame Campan wrote of his appearance—"His straight, unpowdered hair, his round hat, his brown cloth coat, formed a singular contrast with the laced and embroidered coats and perfumed heads of the courtiers of Versailles."

He had an interview with Voltaire, who had expressed a desire to see the illustrious American. Voltaire complimented Dr. Franklin by opening and carrying on the conversation in English.

During the ten months he had been waiting to be recognized by the government of France as the agent of a new nation over the seas, a number of foreign officers had applied to him for letters recommending them to Congress, or to General Washington; and the volume soon swelled to such a size as to be truly embarrassing. The contents of these letters were as various as possible; they set forth the wonderful exploits of the writers, or enclosed certificates and recommendations of men of rank and military commanders. Franklin could only answer to them all that he had no

26*

offices in the army to bestow, and no power to engage officers for the American army, but it was to no purpose. He wrote almost in despair to a friend,—"You can have no idea how I am harassed. All my friends are sought out, and teased to tease me. Great officers of rank in all departments,—ladies, great and small,—besides professed solicitors, worry me from morning till night."

But in the case of the young Marquis de Lafayette he proceeded differently; he recommended him to Congress and his countrymen at once, and, in conjunction with Mr. Deane, signed a letter to Congress, in which it was stated that he (Lafayette) was "gone to America in a ship of his own, accompanied by some officers of distinction, in order to serve in our armies. He is exceedingly beloved, and everybody's good wishes attend him. * * * He has left a beautiful young wife, and, for her sake particularly, we hope that his bravery and ardent desire to distinguish himself will be a little restrained by the General's prudence, so as not to permit his being hazarded much except on some important occasion."

On the 14th of September, 1778, Congress appointed him Minister Plenipotentiary to the French Court. He had well deserved so distinguishing a mark of the public confidence. It was the crowning part of his long public career. He was seventy-two years old; an age when most men think they should be snug at home, perhaps tenants of the chimney corner.

As Minister, his duties became at once very much more weighty than as one of the three commissioners; yet he was able, notwithstanding his age, to perform them with regularity and efficiency. He had political enemies, who let pass no occasion to criticise the manner in which he performed his official duties; but his calm frame of mind and placid temper were not disturbed by their faultfinding. He discharged the offices incumbent on him, at any rate, with such perfect acceptance as to maintain for himself and his country the steady favor of the King and Ministry, who never refused to grant one of his requests, though they were made with embarrassing frequency, and generally pertained to money. It was one of his own admissions afterward, that the Minister for Foreign Affairs, Count de Vergennes, always fulfilled his promises; and that not one of the large number of drafts which were drawn on him by Congress, during the war, was allowed to go to protest, or to pass the time of payment.

He received several proposals, while **Minister**, to act as mediator for a peace between **the mother country** and the colonies, **on** condition that America should concede certain commercial privileges to **England** which she did **not** to France; but that sort of condition was **entirely out of the** question. He was addressed, also, **on** the subject by a secret agent under **an** assumed name, who laid before him a plan of reconciliation, and a form of government for America in the future. The writer took occasion to disparage France **as much** as he could, and to **assure** Franklin that **America** would find her **fickle and false**; and then, as if to impress Franklin with the **power and** determination of **England, he added,** that Parliament would never acknowledge the independence **of the colonies, nor would** the people of England ever submit to **such an act.** He declared that the **British title** to the empire was perfect, and that the present generation, and their successors after them, would insist upon that title forever. Franklin always thought this secret agent of the British government was really in Paris all the time, though he dated his letter from Brussels. And supposing that he was acting in the interest of the British Ministry, he replied in a manner which he thought would best meet the case. The answer is one of his finest specimens of combined ridicule, sarcasm, pungency, and strong thought.

While serving in a public and political capacity, Franklin had drawn to him a large number of friends, composed of the most distinguished men not only of Paris but of France; men known in scientific, literary, and political circles above the other men of their time. When he attended the meetings of the French Academy, he was always received by the members with most marked attention.

He had his thoughts about him always for inventions, improvements, and plans of whatever sort, which were calculated, as he believed, to prove of benefit to the human race. He was in all respects a man of philanthropy and progress. The famous Captain Cook being about to return from a voyage of discovery, Dr. Franklin sent a circular letter to the captains of American cruisers, requesting them not to capture, or even to detain, much less to plunder the vessel of anything which they might find on board, in case they should fall in with it. Captain Cook being an Englishman, and Franklin being Foreign Minister of a power with which England was then at war, an act of such a character could not go without its influence; and accordingly, when Captain Cook's "Voyage" was published, the Board of Admiralty sent a copy to Dr. Franklin, accompanied with a letter from Lord Howe which informed him that it was presented with the King's personal approval. A medal, struck in honor of Captain Cook by the Royal Society, was also sent him.

Paul Jones, the "father of the American Navy," likewise presented himself before him, in connection with a plan which had been formed for fitting out a squadron of vessels to make a descent on the coast of England. There was to be a land force connected with the expedition, which Lafayette would command; Jones would be in command of the squadron. This scheme, however, fell through. Jones soon after won immortal renown by fighting the frigate Serapis with the Bon Homme Richard, off the English coast; the affairs of his cruise required adjustment afterwards, especially his trouble with the French Captain Landais, who was second in command; and this delicate business devolved upon Dr. Franklin.

With all his public duties and his social demands, he never neglected the pursuit of his studies in philosophy. Sir Humphrey Davy says of some of his researches and writings—"By very small means he established very grand truths. * * * He has written equally for the uninitiated and for the philosopher; and he has rendered his details amusing as well as perspicuous, elegant as well as simple. Science appears in his language in a dress wonderfully decorous, the best adapted to display her native loveliness. He has in no instance exhibited that false dignity by which philosophy is kept aloof from common applications; and he has sought rather to make her a useful inmate and servant in the common habitations of man, than to preserve her merely as an object of admiration in temples and palaces." Higher praise could not be written. It was Franklin's part to bring down the mysteries of science to the comprehension of the people.

While still Minister to France, and after he had been approached by a British agent, a member of Parliament, on the subject of reconciling the colonies with the mother country even at the expense of the friendship of France, the Englishman wrote him, just as he was leaving Paris for London,—"If tempestuous times should come, take care of your own safety; events are uncertain, and men are capricious." Franklin replied to him,—"I

thank you for your kind caution; but, having
nearly finished a long life, I set but little value
upon what remains of it. Like a draper, when
one chaffers with him for a remnant, I am ready
to say, 'As it is only a fag end, I will not differ
with you about it; take it for what you please.'
Perhaps the best use such an old fellow can be put
to, is to make a martyr of him."

The respect paid to Franklin by the French people, as well as by the Court and the men of letters, was well calculated to gratify even the vanity
of the young nation which he represented. His
portraits and medals were to be seen everywhere.
Over and around his head on the medals was impressed the noble, but wholly deserved, inscription
of Turgot,—"Eripuit cœlo fulmen, sceptrumque
tyrannis:"—which is translated,—"He snatched
the lightning from heaven, and the sceptre from
tyrants."

There were stories set on foot, after a time, that
he was too compliant to the French Court, and
that America would fare better if she put on a
more bold manner. Mr. John Adams, afterwards
Minister to Great Britain, was of this opinion.
The talk that was made over it soon led to suggestions in Congress whether another might not

with advantage be appointed to Dr. Franklin's place. The French Minister in the United States, M. De la Luzerne, wrote to Count de Vergennes, Foreign Minister of France,—"Congress is filled with intrigues and cabals respecting the recall of Dr. Franklin, which the delegates from Massachusetts insist on by all sorts of means." The Count wrote back in reply,—"If you are questioned respecting our opinion of Dr. Franklin, you may say, without hesitation, that we esteem him as much for his patriotism as for the wisdom of his conduct. * * * We are of opinion that his recall would be very inconvenient in the present state of things, and it would be the more disagreeable to us, inasmuch as he would perhaps be succeeded by a character unquiet, exacting, difficult, and less ardently attached to the cause of his country."

Dr. Franklin was of the last service to the United States in procuring loans of money with which to carry on the war. The French government had loaned us already about three millions of livres a year. In 1781, he increased that loan to four millions, besides a subsidy of six millions, which was a "gift outright to America." Even after that, Col. Laurens came over to Paris to solicit further aid still. Dr. Franklin joined with

27

him in making the request, and was to a degree successful. The King could do nothing more from the government treasury, but he promised to guarantee the interest of a loan in Holland, the debt not to exceed ten millions of livres.

He was at this time seventy-five years old, and he formed his plans to withdraw from public life altogether. In writing to the President of Congress on the subject, he said,—"I have passed my seventy-fifth year; and I find that the long and severe fit of the gout, which I had the last winter, has shaken me exceedingly, and I am yet far from having recovered the bodily strength I before enjoyed. I do not know that my mental faculties are impaired; perhaps I shall be the last to discover that; but I am sensible of great diminution in my activity. * * * I find, also, that the business is too heavy for me, and too confining. The constant attendance at home, which is necessary for receiving and accepting your bills of exchange, to answer letters, and perform other parts of my employment, prevents my taking the air and exercise which my annual journeys formerly used to afford me, and which contributed much to the preservation of my health."

He had been in public life now for fifty years;

and he confessed that he had, in that time, enjoyed honor enough to satisfy any reasonable ambition. He craved nothing but repose and rest; and he hoped Congress would at once grant his request and send some one else to take his place. He did not propose, however, to return home at once, for the fatigues of the last sea voyage had nearly overcome his strength; but he thought he would stay in France until after peace was declared, and perhaps for the remainder of his life. Whatever experience he had already gained there, he was ready to turn over to his successor.

Congress was not ready to listen to his proposal. That body was just making up a commission to negotiate a peace with Great Britain,—the surrender of Cornwallis at Yorktown having virtually decided the contest,—and Dr. Franklin was named with four other gentlemen to join Mr. Adams. He therefore continued to hold his office. Having been already addressed in the British interest on the subject of a reconciliation, he was now plied with insidious proposals most industriously. They tried to influence him to agree, for one thing, on a ten years' truce, during which America was not to assist France, while England was to carry on war against that power. Franklin denounced such a proposal as the depth of perfidy. To sunder the ties that held France and the United States together, England was ready to make the last endeavor. She offered tempting baits for that purpose alike to France and the United States; but none of them were efficient to work the result desired. The entire independence of the United States was the great matter which both were resolved to secure.

CHAPTER XIV.

CLOSE OF HIS CAREER.

HIS domestic relations at the pleasant little village of Passy were of the most delightful character. The family of M. Brillon, in which he made his home, treated him as one of their own number, and with sentiments of affectionate reverence. The neighbors all delighted in his genial society, and he was an object of universal love.

The subject of animal magnetism came up before the public mind, during the latter part of Dr. Franklin's mission, and he gave much attention to it as one of the wonders of the time; but he was not led to put any faith in its reality and truth as a new discovery.

The people of England having become at length tired of the war, they clamored for its termination; and the ministry were obliged to yield. In order

27*

to meet the changed aspect of affairs, Congress
had promptly appointed the five commissioners
spoken of, Dr. Franklin being one, to meet at
Paris and be ready to receive any proposals which
the British ministry might be disposed to make.
There were four leading points insisted on by
Congress:—1st, the independence of the United
States; 2d, a settlement of the boundaries between
the remaining British colonies and the United
States; 3d, a contraction of the boundaries of
Canada to their condition before the bill which
was passed by Parliament for the punishment of
Massachusetts; and, 4th, the free use of the New-
foundland Banks for fishing.

These points were all discussed at great length,
after the negotiating parties were met. The
British commission labored hard to have this
point yielded, and that point modified; but the
American commissioners were inflexible. The
articles being all arranged, they were signed on
the 30th of November, 1782, at Paris, Franklin
being seventy-six years of age at the time. This
body of an agreement was the basis of the treaty
which was afterwards concluded, and likewise
signed at Paris, on the 3d day of September, 1783.
This transaction was the token of the close of the

Revolution, and of the birth of a new nation into the world.

Dr. Franklin wrote to a friend concerning this event in history, that it was one he hardly expected to live to see. "A few years of peace," said he, "well improved, will restore and increase our strength; but our future safety will depend on our union and our virtue."

The remainder of his residence in France, after the signing of the treaty of peace with Great Britain, was but a continuation of the agreeable life he had been leading there from the first. As Minister, the last public act of his career was putting his hand to a treaty with Prussia, which he did in 1785.

Congress was at last ready to yield to his solicitations to be relieved of his official position, and sent over Mr. Thomas Jefferson to Paris to succeed him at the Court of Versailles. He had lived for eight and a half years in France, and served his countrymen with fidelity and singleness of purpose. Leaving his native land when she had only resolved on independence, it was his earnest wish to return and witness the change in her condition. If he should be so fortunate as to cross

the seas in safety, he hoped to pass the short
remainder of his life in tranquillity and peace.

After taking an affectionate and impressive
leave of his numerous friends, he embarked at
Havre for Southampton on the last of July, 1785;
and after a very brief stay in England, set sail for
the United States. In his Journal is to be found
the following record of his arrival on his native
shores :—

" WEDNESDAY, SEPTEMBER 14TH.—With the flood
in the morning, came a light breeze, which brought
us above Gloucester Point, in full view of dear
Philadelphia! when we again cast anchor to wait
for the health officer, who, having made his visit,
and finding no sickness, gave us leave to land.
My son-in-law came in a boat to us; we landed at
Market street wharf, where we were received by
a crowd of people, with huzzas, and accompanied
with acclamations quite to my door. Found my
family well. God be praised for his mercies !"

He at once went to live with his daughter, his
wife being some time dead. "I am again surrounded by my friends," wrote he to another,
"with a fine family of grand-children about my
knees, and an affectionate, good daughter and
son-in-law to take care of me." It was his sincere

wish, after having seen fifty years of public service, to be allowed the remainder of his days for repose and reflection; but the needs of his countrymen hardly allowed that; he was in perpetual demand, if not in positive action, then in council.

Hardly had he become settled once more in his new domestic state, before he was elected to the Supreme Executive Council of Pennsylvania. After that, he was made President of the province, —an office equal to that of Governor. Aged as he was, he still felt himself so completely in possession of his faculties as not to hesitate about assuming the new gifts imposed on him. He shrank from nothing to which he was adequate. To the last, his faculties were bright and elastic.

As President, he could hold the office for three years; and for the succeeding *four years* he would be ineligible. While yet in possession of this office, he was likewise elected a member of the convention for framing a Constitution of the United States, which assembled in Philadelphia, in May, 1787. At that time he was in his eighty-second year! Men of that age do not, now-a-days, go about such weighty business as framing the fundamental law for a country. One is surprised to find how vigorous his mind was, and how tenacious still of work. Long after the time when other men are generally through their life-work, and their lives also, Dr. Franklin was occupied with a task which would have challenged the employment of the energy of their youth. He made short but pithy speeches before the Convention on the several points debated; and, after the work was finished in that body, lent his further efforts to make the Constitution acceptable to his countrymen. He did not approve of every article of that great instrument himself; but he yielded to the opinions and sentiments of others, in return for their yielding in a degree to his own.

His life, from this time, may be considered rather a private than a public one. He lived, at that period, in Market street; his house was described as standing "up a court, at some distance from the street." Dr. Cutler, of Massachusetts, a famous botanist, who visited him at home in his old age, wrote in his journal of the sage,—"We found him in his garden, sitting upon a grass plot, under a very large mulberry tree, (this was in July, 1787) with several other gentlemen and two or three ladies. When Mr. Gerry introduced me, he rose from his chair, took me by the hand, expressed his joy at seeing me, welcomed me to the

city, and begged me to seat myself close to him.
His voice was low, but his countenance open,
frank, and pleasing. I delivered to him my letters.
After he had read them, he took me again by the
hand, and, with the usual compliments, introduced
me to the other gentlemen, who were most of them
members of the Convention.

"Here we entered into a free conversation, and
spent our time most agreeably, until it was quite
dark. The tea-table was spread under the tree;
and Mrs. Bache, who is the only daughter (Sarah)
of the Doctor, and lives with him, served it out to
the company. She had three of her children
about her. They seemed to be exceedingly fond
of their grandpapa"

"After it was dark, we went into the house, and
he invited me into his library, which is likewise
his study. It is a very large chamber, and high-
studded. The walls are covered with book-shelves,
filled with books; besides, there are four large
alcoves, extending two-thirds the length of the
chamber, filled in the same manner. * * * He
showed us a glass machine for exhibiting the
circulation of the blood in the arteries and veins
of the human body. * * * Another great
curiosity was a rolling press, for taking the copies

of letters, or any other writing. * * * He also showed us his long artificial *arm and hand*, for taking down and putting up books on high shelves, which are out of reach ; and his great arm-chair, with rockers, and a large fan placed over it, with which he fans himself, keeps off the flies, &c., while he sits reading, with only a small motion of the feet. * * * Over his mantel, he has a prodigious number of medals, busts, and casts in wax, or plaster of Paris, which are the effigies of the most noted characters in Europe."

His talk was chiefly on science, and especially on philosophy. The rest of the company talked politics. His visitor records that his conversation betrayed extensive knowledge, a bright and ready memory, and a perfect clearness of all the mental faculties, notwithstanding his age. His manners were easy, and calculated to make all persons contented in his presence. His vein of humor showed just as freshly as in earlier days. He talked and chatted with great freedom, keeping the conversation always alive.

He was drawing near, however, to the close of his long and useful life. There was little else for him to do in the world. His days were well spent. During the last two or three years of his life he was a continual sufferer from inward pain, which gave him warning, perhaps, of his end. But the end was still delayed. Not until 1790, in the month of April, was he assailed with the disease which was the immediate cause of his decease. He had been obliged to keep his bed, for the greater part of a twelvemonth previously; and, in the intervals of his pain, he entertained himself with reading and his friends with conversation. His faculties were all this time perfectly clear, and his kindness and goodness of heart as much to be remarked as ever. He originated pleasantries after the old way, and was as ready as formerly with his anecdotes.

A little more than two weeks before his death, he was overtaken with feverish symptoms, which attracted no special attention for two or three days; but he soon afterward was afflicted with a cough, and his breathing became laborious. Once or twice he groaned, which drew from him the remark that he was afraid he did not bear the pain as he ought. He expressed his gratitude for the many blessings he had received at the hands of Heaven, that he had been raised from such a low and small beginning to his high rank and consideration among men. He could not but be-

28

lieve that his present afflictions were sent to wean him from a world in which he was no longer fit to act the part assigned him.

For five days in all, he lay in this state; at the end of which time his pain and all difficulty of breathing had left him. His friends even felt encouraged that his life would be prolonged. But it was a vain hope. A trouble of the lungs made itself apparent now, from which his respiration gradually became so oppressed as to be checked altogether. He finally passed away in a lethargic state, at eleven o'clock at night, on the 17th of April, 1790. He had reached the advanced age of eighty-four years and three months.

The intelligence of his death called forth expressions of sorrow and sympathy alike from America and Europe. Congress passed resolutions appropriate to the event, and so did the National Assembly of France. Other bodies, both scientific and political, added their testimony to the universal appreciation of his life and character.

Of his religious views many inquiries have been made, and assertions of his lack of faith in Divine Power have been in circulation. Skeptics have claimed him as belonging to their class, and sticklers for mere creeds have discarded him as of no worth to them. That Franklin was a profoundly *religious* man, his long life abundantly attests. Only five weeks before his death, he answered to the questions of Dr. Stiles, President of Yale College,—"I believe in one God, the Creator of the universe; that he governs it by his Providence; that he ought to be worshipped; that the most acceptable service we can render to Him is doing good to His other children; that the soul of man is immortal, and will be treated with justice in another life respecting its conduct in this. * * * As to Jesus of Nazareth, my opinion of whom you particularly desire, I think his system of morals and his religion, as he left them to us, the best the world ever saw, or is like to see; but I apprehend it has received various corrupting changes, and I have, with most of the present Dissenters in England, some doubts as to his divinity; though it is a question I do not dogmatize upon, having never studied it."

In none of his writings does Franklin say aught against religion, but rather inculcates it as a rule for the life. He kept the company of such a man as Whitfield, who used to lodge at his house. He was a liberal contributor to the building of churches and the support of ministers. He early in life composed a book of prayers; and he abridged the Book of Common Prayer, to which he wrote a Preface. While in France, a skeptical writer, supposed to be Thomas Paine, showed him his work against religion in manuscript; and Franklin advised him to burn it. In his letter of advice to his daughter, written while waiting on board ship before sailing for England, he inculcated the duty of attending divine worship with regularity.

In the Convention for framing the Constitution, too, after that body had been in session some four or five weeks, it being apparently impossible to make any headway with business, he rose and proposed that the daily sessions be opened with prayer. He said, in support of his motion,—"In the beginning of the contest with Britain, when we were sensible of danger, we had daily prayers in this room for divine protection. Our prayers, sir, were heard; and they were graciously answered. * * * And have we now forgotten that powerful Friend? or do we imagine we no longer need his assistance? I have lived, sir, a long time: and, the longer I live, the more convincing proofs I see of this truth, that God governs in the affairs of men. And, if a sparrow cannot fall to the ground without his notice, is it probable that an empire can rise without his aid? We have been assured, sir, that, 'except the Lord build the house, they labor in vain that build it.' I firmly believe this; and I also believe, that, without his concurring aid, we shall succeed in this political building no better than the builders of Babel." His motion was not adopted, however, the Convention seeming to think, with the exception of three or four members, that prayers were "unnecessary."

Dr. Franklin was ever a friend and advocate of the cause of education. He renewed, in the last days of his life, the earnestness with which he set about the establishment of the Academy in Philadelphia, some forty years before. But he advocated the study of the English, and other modern tongues, before putting the learner upon the dead languages. To stop in this day to study Greek and Latin he thought as useless as to wear broad cuffs with buttons, after gloves began to be worn, and to continue the use of the cocked hat after umbrellas were introduced.

In the relief of his pains, he busied himself with writing a variety of short papers, showing that his mental vigor and freshness still remained. One

28*

of these papers was upon the license of the press, in assailing individuals; another compared the conduct of the anti-Federalists to that of the Jews; and he also gave some little time to the writing of his own memoirs, which he hoped, while in Europe, to have leisure to finish on settling down once more at home. He likewise drew up a plan for improving the condition of the free blacks. Indeed, it is said that the last public act of his life was to sign his name, as President of the Abolition Society of Pennsylvania, to a memorial of the society to Congress; and the last paper he ever wrote was upon that particular topic. The paper in question was a sort of parody of a speech by a member of Congress from Georgia, in favor of negro slavery. Dr. Franklin represents Sidi Mehemet Ibrahim as making a speech in the divan of Algiers, in opposition to the petition of a sect called *Erika*, who desired the abolition of piracy and slavery. Ibrahim brings forward exactly the same arguments and sentiments in his speech, in favor of enslaving Europeans, that had been used by the Georgia member of Congress.

He was a warm personal friend of Washington to the last. He wrote him, in September of the year preceding his death, congratulating him on the growing strength of the new government under his personal administration; and he went on to say—"For my own personal ease, I should have died two years ago; but, though those years have been spent in excruciating pain, I am pleased that I have lived them, since they have brought me to see our present situation. I am now finishing my eighty-fourth year, and probably with it my career in this life; but in whatever state of existence I am placed hereafter, if I retain any memory of what has passed here, I shall with it retain the esteem, respect, and affection, with which I have long been, my dear friend, yours most sincerely." Franklin was the first person whom Washington called on, when he came from his farm in Virginia to take his seat in the Convention which framed the Constitution; and he was just as attentive, on passing through Philadelphia afterwards, to be invested in New York with the august Presidential office.

The funeral services over the body of Dr. Franklin were attended by more than twenty thousand persons. The bells of the city were all muffled and tolled. The flags on the shipping were hung at half-mast. And when the rites of sepulture were over, the discharge of cannon made the fact impressive to the hearts of all who heard their thunders. The sage and philosopher was buried by the side of his wife, in the Christ Church Cemetery, of Philadelphia. Both graves are covered with a slab of marble, perfectly plain, as he had directed in his will; and the only inscription upon the same was the record of their names and the year of his decease. Over the place of his birth, in Boston, in Milk Street, has been erected a fine granite store, on the high brow of which are chiselled the two or three words that mark that as the spot of Franklin's nativity. The city of Boston has erected a fine bronze statue of him in City Hall Square, where one may gaze at the significant attitude of the philosopher to his heart's content and improvement. What is a little remarkable about the expression of the face, if it were a happy accident on the part of the designer, one side of it betrays the character of the philosopher and sage, and the other the worldly-wise man and the man of shrewd humor.

In person, Dr. Franklin was of what is styled a strong build, and short rather than tall. He grew a little fleshy as he grew older. His complexion was light, and his eyes were of that inevitable gray which is a puzzle to all other eyes

for the depth and variety of its expression. He
was inclined to be silent in a mixed company, but
in the presence of his friends he was genial and
free. His conversation was frank and winning,
and enriched with the results of his experience
and observation, his humor and shrewd sagacity,
his engaging anecdotes and sensible reflections.
He possessed a sound judgment, remarkable sagacity, and held calm command at all times over
his passions. What secured for him success in
whatever he set about, he was wise enough never
to let either his vanity or his prejudices stand in
his way; he was never in his own light. With
such balance of his faculties, he was able to direct
them upon any single object, and touch the results
he aimed at. For humanity and genuine philanthropy, no American can be placed before him;
he was always doing good, his long life through,
by precept, by example, and with such means as
a kind Providence had placed at the disposal of
his benevolence.

THE END.

www.ingramcontent.com/pod-product-compliance
Lightning Source LLC
Chambersburg PA
CBHW020941030726
47496CB00005B/1293